A Sinful Mistake

Miss Fortune World (A Miss Prim & Proper Mystery), Volume 4

Caroline Mickelson

Published by J&R Fan Fiction, 2018.

A SINFUL MISTAKE

First edition. August 16, 2018.

ISBN: 979-8201566517

Written by Caroline Mickelson.

Chapter One

"NO. NOT FOR ALL THE banana pudding in the world." I tore my gaze from the hideous bright neon green pair of running shoes that my Aunt Ida Belle was holding and looked her straight in the eye. "It's not happening."

She lifted an eyebrow. "Church service starts in twenty minutes, Stephanie," she said. "You're wasting our time."

I took a deep breath to fortify myself for the fight ahead. I'd only known my great-aunt Ida Belle for a couple of weeks. But I'd learned enough about her to know that she was formidable. Iron curtain formidable. However, she was both my hostess and an elder relative, so I knew that proper manners dictated I be amenable to her suggestions. But there was no way I was going to ruin my outfit, not to mention my reputation in Sinful, by donning the footwear she was attempting to thrust upon me. "I'm sorry, Aunt Ida Belle, but I simply will not wear anything so ugly. Ever. Under any circumstances." I crossed my arms over chest, ready to hold my ground until the bitter end. "Period. End of conversation."

"So, that's a maybe?" Gertie asked, a hopeful expression on her wrinkled face as she looked between us. She clapped her hands together. "Hot damn, we're making progress."

"Gertie, look at what I'm wearing." I waved a hand over my white linen sheath dress, which was accessorized with my signature string of pearls and a delicate gold bracelet. "It would be an absolute crime to replace these—" I pointed to my kitten heeled white leather sandals and then to the offending sneakers that my aunt held, "—with those athletic monstrosities."

Gertie's eyebrows knit together. "Huh, shows what I know. I don't remember any laws being passed that prohibited wearing ugly shoes on a Sunday." Her face broke into a wide smile. "Hot dog, that means we can get Celia arrested because her shoes are always as ugly as a baboon's butt."

"I think what Stephanie means is that it would be a crime against fashion." Fortune, an ex-beauty queen and ex-librarian, as well as the third member of the unholy alliance that comprised my Aunt Ida Belle's inner circle, flashed me a sympathetic smile.

Like myself, Fortune was several decades younger than my great-aunt and Gertie. She was also a Yankee and a relative newcomer to Sinful, although that's where the similarities between us ended. Fortune had a predisposition toward wearing yoga pants and plain cotton t-shirts, she possessed an encyclopedic knowledge of assault weapons, and she had a tendency to drink beer straight out of the bottle. But this wasn't what made me slightly weary of her. Something was off with her story that she was spending the summer in Sinful, Louisiana, to catalog her recently deceased aunt's possessions. As far as I could tell after spending a great deal of time in her company, she hadn't inventoried anything in the last couple of weeks.

Whatever Fortune was doing in this little bayou town, it wasn't settling an estate. But then the same question could well be asked of me. What was I doing in Sinful? When I'd first arrived several weeks ago, that would have been a simple question to answer. I was hiding from a Russian mob family because they'd put a hit out on me. But that little kerfuffle had since been settled and it was now safe for me to return to my home and my job back in Boston.

Yet here I was, with no return bus ticket in hand. This had to do in great part with my growing attachment to my Aunt Ida Belle and her friends, but it also had more than a little something to do with an exciting and sexy FBI Agent named Kase Mayeux I'd met soon after I arrived.

So, really, who was I to question Fortune's reasons for being in Sinful?

"Earth to Stephanie." Gertie waved a hand in front of my face. "Tick, tock. Time's a wastin', girl. We need to know if you're in."

I shook my head to clear my thoughts. It didn't pay to gather wool in front of these ladies. Not the way they went from zero to flat out crazy in thirty seconds or less. "Am I in what?"

"In it to win it," Gertie said, her voice hopeful.

"Win what precisely?" There was no way I was going to agree to anything without first understanding exactly what they were talking about. I could well end up mud wrestling on Main Street if I didn't keep my wits about me.

"Banana pudding!" Gertie exclaimed, holding up her two hands for Fortune and Ida Belle to high five.

I stared at the three of them as if they'd lost their minds. "I'm confused. Are we going to church to confess our sins and pray for our salvation, or are we going so that we can run a race afterward in the hopes of winning banana pudding? Because, to my mind, that really isn't a legitimate choice."

"You're right." My Aunt Ida Belle slipped a hand under my elbow and propelled me toward the front door. "There's not much of a choice when it comes down to it."

I eyed her suspiciously as we stepped out onto her front porch. "There isn't?"

"No," Gertie chimed in as she slipped past us and ran down the steps toward her rusted out old Cadillac. "Banana pudding all the way!"

Fortune followed me outside. "You might as well go along with their plans, it's easier that way."

"Why can't you race?" I asked. "You're in better shape than I am." I resisted the urge to mention that her footwear, a pair of well worn Huarache sandals, were just as ugly as the running shoes my great-aunt was trying to get me to wear. In fact, the switch might be a bit of an upgrade.

"My knees are sore from all the running I've been doing lately. I'm just going to baby them for a few days."

Not to sound callous, but I didn't see why she couldn't start babying them tomorrow.

Gertie opened the Cadillac's rear passenger door and motioned for me to get in, which I did. "Just don't turn all prim on us," she said.

Aunt Ida Belle slid in the front passenger side, slammed the door shut, and turned back to fix a stern look on me. "And don't go getting all proper, either."

But their instructions fell on deaf ears. Prim and proper defined me. Literally. I, Stephanie St. James, am a manners columnist for the Boston Daily News.

Miss Prim & Proper is my name, etiquette is my game.

Gertie's Caddy roared to life and I grabbed onto the back of the driver's seat in front of me. I'd learned the hard way that Gertie drove like a maniac. On a good day. On her bad days, she drove like a certified lunatic menace. As we peeled out of the driveway and tore off toward the center of town, I realized this was one of her bad days.

And I also wondered, not for the first time this week, if I wouldn't perhaps be just a bit safer in Boston.

THE SINFUL BAPTIST Church was the farthest thing from sinful imaginable. I struggled to stay awake as Pastor Don droned on about a biblical lesson that made no sense whatsoever. Something about Noah allowing David and Goliath on the ark. I'm not even wholly convinced that he understood what he was preaching. As the service wore on, and my eyelids grew heavy, I snuck a look at my companions.

Fortune sat staring straight ahead, her expression inscrutable. If I didn't know better, I'd have sworn she was meditating. Or sleeping with her eyes open. Gertie sat beside her, tapping out the refrain to *Three Blind Mice* with the toes of her shoes. Sandwiched between us was Aunt Ida Belle.

They'd insisted we occupy the last row and that I sit in the aisle seat nearest the doors that led out onto Main Street. Clearly, they were very confident that I'd jump out of my seat the minute service was over and run down the street toward Francine's Diner as if my very life depended on it.

I glanced down at my sandals, glad that I'd packed them when I'd fled Boston. I'd packed my suitcase in a terrible hurry, but death threat or no death threat, outfits had to be coordinated. Dressing as fashionably as possible was staying true to who I was as a person.

But being a considerate houseguest was integral to my integrity as well. I bit my lip and looked around the church. Had Gertie been right when she'd claimed that the rows full of elderly ladies, long standing members of the Sinful Ladies Society, were counting on me to win the race?

I was far from athletic. True, I played tennis well enough to hold my head high at the country club but that was about it. As a matter of fact, I preferred to play doubles so I'd have less court to cover. I just wasn't fond of sports.

On the other hand, I'd developed a certain fondness for my new friends, so perhaps I should give the race a try. After all, wasn't it my Christian duty to assist the elderly? The hungry? The weak?

I glanced over my shoulder at the double wooden doors.

"The Lord calls on us to be neighborly," Pastor Don intoned.

I wondered about the competition. How fast could the Catholics run if they were weighed down with Eucharist? Bread and wine weren't an ideal way to prepare for a race.

"He calls on us to make sacrifices for those in need—"

My great-aunt's friends were in need of nourishment, surely. Why shouldn't it be the best banana pudding in Louisiana? They deserved that much.

"Go forth in peace—"

I glanced over at Aunt Ida Belle. I wasn't surprised to see that she was watching me intently. I gave her an imperceptible nod. I'd do it. I'd run the silly race and do my level best to reach Francine's Diner before anyone else. A wide smile stretched across her wrinkled face as she pulled the running shoes from the plastic grocery bag beside her.

Hesitating only briefly, I took them. I don't think anyone noticed that I slipped my sandals off and put the green monstrosities on in their place. Out of the corner of my eye, I saw Gertie flash me a thumbs up. Her response, as well as Aunt Ida Belle's obvious approval of my choice, made me feel like I'd just been inducted into a club for the super cool kids.

Now all I had to do was run down the street in the most undignified manner imaginable, burst into Francine's diner, and fling myself into a seat before anyone else did.

"—and keep God's love alive in your heart."

The words were barely out of Pastor Don's mouth before Aunt Ida Belle elbowed me. "Go," she hissed. "And don't take any prisoners."

I jumped to my feet and bolted out through the front doors. Despite the bright sunlight, I immediately saw that this wasn't a one-woman race. The doors to Sinful's Catholic Church were open and three women were already beating a path to Francine's.

"Run, Stephanie, run," Gertie shouted. "Beat those old buzzards."

Heeding her words, I threw decorum to the wind and broke into a full-on sprint. I managed to duck and weave through a trio of Catholic ladies. The fact that I overtook them was attributable to their advanced age rather than a testament to my athletic prowess. Still, it was a winner-take-all race.

One runner pulled ahead of me but only by an arm's length. I sucked in a lungful of humid air and redoubled my efforts. I glanced over. My opponent was none other than Celia Arceneaux. This was a woman I wouldn't mind leaving in the dust, but my word, for a woman of her years and bulk, she certainly could run. I had to do something to slow her down.

"Celia," I called out to her, "your hair piece is slipping."

My words had the desired effect. Celia slowed her pace, lifted her hands to her hair, and anxiously patted her head to search for loose bobby pins. I shot past her, pleased that my hunch that all those sausage curls weren't hers had paid off. As I reached the door to Francine's, I heard her howl in outrage. I yanked the door open and flew inside.

"Hurry, just sit anywhere," Ally directed me. "Get off your feet. It doesn't matter where."

I plopped into the booth nearest me. "That's it? We win?"

Ally, a part-time waitress and good friend of my great aunt and her friends, grinned. "That's it. All you have to do now is face the wrath of Aunt Celia."

In unison, we both looked out through the diner's large window pane. A red-faced Celia was fast making a beeline for the door.

I knew I should feel embarrassed by racing through town like an eight-year-old on summer vacation but, in truth, I felt downright jubilant. I'd kept the faith, run the race, and secured banana pudding for the Sinful Ladies Society. Not bad for the new girl in town.

"Just remember, Celia's more bark than bite," Francine called from the cash register where she stood counting out cash. "Don't let her get to you."

Francine was right, Celia was all bark. It didn't take more than a few seconds of listening to her rant and rave for me to remember why I preferred cats to dogs. The yapping - how did people stand it?

Gertie approached our booth with both fists pumping the air. "Whoo hoo! Wait until old bossy-pants Madam 'Never Gonna Be Mayor' finds out we won." She drew to a stop beside the table and feigned shock at seeing Celia. "Oh, I didn't see you there, Celia. Have you come to praise Sinful's new champion?"

"Shut up, Gertie." Celia turned to look at Fortune and Aunt Ida Belle, who had just arrived. "Well, if it isn't a meeting of the Yankee minds. I tell you, I don't know what this world is coming to."

Aunt Ida Belle slid in the booth next to me. "Shove off, Celia."

Never one to mince words, my Aunt Ida Belle.

"Trust me, I don't want to spend a moment more in your company than I have to." She frowned at me. "Miss Prim & Proper, huh? Tearing through the streets of our town in your Sunday finest? For shame."

Gertie and Fortune slid into the opposite side of the booth. "Go away, Celia," Fortune said. "You've said your piece."

At Fortune's use of the word 'piece', Gertie howled with laughter.

Celia's face turned bright red. "I will have you know that I don't wear a hair piece. You two Yankees should go back where you came from, and you two Yankee lovers are a disgrace to southern womanhood." When no one took the bait, she turned to go, but then stopped. A smug expression replaced her look of indignation. "There's just one more thing." She reached into her pink faux-leather handbag and rustled around. "Gertie, I have your receipt for your unpaid parking tickets." She pulled out an envelope and slapped it in the middle of the table. "It was smart of you to pay up seeing as how you've decided to leave town."

Chapter Two

IT WAS AS IF CELIA'S words turned us all to stone.

We sat in stunned silence. Aunt Ida Belle didn't even blink. It took the arrival of Francine with our bowls of banana pudding to break through the shock that had descended over our table.

"Nice bit of running you did, Stephanie," Francine said as she slid my bowl in front of me. "I know the Sinful Ladies thank you."

"They're most welcome," I said as if on auto-pilot. My manners rarely deserted me, even if my wits did. I picked up my spoon but was unable to make myself partake of the prize in front of me. I replaced my utensil on the Formica table top.

Francine frowned. "Something wrong here, ladies?"

I looked at Aunt Ida Belle but she remained uncharacteristically quiet. Gertie's eyes were downcast, which, I will say, did little to reassure me that Celia had just been stirring up trouble. Fortune, however, met my gaze. She shook her head nearly imperceptibly, as if to suggest I not repeat Celia's bombshell. I remained silent.

"Nope, nothing's wrong here," Fortune said. She picked up her spoon. "Is there, Stephanie?"

I took the cue and dipped my spoon into the banana pudding. "Everything's fine, thank you, Francine." I then took my first taste of the famous pudding. Emotional devastation aside, I was able to fully appreciate the flavor explosion. I had no doubt I was experiencing a taste of the finest banana pudding south of the Mason-Dixon line. I told our hostess so.

"South of the line?" Francine scoffed. "Don't try to convince me that you've tasted finer pudding than mine up north." She shook her head. "Yankees," she muttered as she wandered back toward the kitchen.

Once we were alone, Fortune turned her attention to Gertie. "Please tell us that Celia was just blowing smoke."

Gertie shrugged without looking up. "Doesn't she always?"

"That's not an answer." Fortune's voice was no-nonsense. "Let's try this again. What was Celia talking about?"

Gertie picked up her fork and began tapping it on the table. "Nothing, I told you."

Aunt Ida Belle shot her a look of pure frustration. "You're going to do it, aren't you?" When Gertie didn't answer, or even look up, she cursed under her breath. "You old fool."

I lifted another spoonful of banana pudding to my lips. What on earth was going on? Gertie looked both defiant and contrite. Aunt Ida Belle appeared angry, and yet wounded. I glanced at Fortune. My guess was that she was as confused as I was. I took another bite, justifying that it was socially acceptable to eat under the rather tense circumstances because I didn't know what to say.

We sat in uncomfortable silence for several more moments before Fortune slid out of the booth and headed to the register. She returned with three take-out containers, which she made short order of filling. As inconspicuously as possible, I scraped the last of my pudding onto my spoon and savored it. Under any other circumstances I would be asking how we planned to spend the remainder of the day but I held my tongue. Clearly, our highest priority was to sort this out.

Whatever this was.

"I don't have to take this abuse," Gertie blurted out. She elbowed Fortune to let her out of the booth. "I'm old enough to do what I want but still young enough to enjoy life." With that rather odd pronouncement, she slung her purse up onto her shoulder and took off for the door.

I stood, assuming we were going to follow her, after all, she was the one with the car, but when neither my great-aunt nor Fortune made a move to follow her, I sat back down. We listened as Gertie fired up the Caddy and peeled out onto Main Street as if she were fleeing a heist. I sighed. It looked as if we would be walking home. At least I had sneakers on.

Fortune was the first to break the silence. "You seem to know what this is all about, Ida Belle. Care to enlighten Stephanie and me?"

Aunt Ida Belle blew out a long breath. "The old biddy has finally lost her mind. Gone loco." She shook her head in disgust. "I saw the signs but I couldn't believe anyone would be that stupid. Especially not Gertie."

"I'm sorry, Aunt Ida Belle, but I'm completely lost. What exactly has Gertie done?"

"She's made a fool out of herself, that's what."

Now this was a tricky thing to respond to without being offensive because, quite frankly, Gertie has been known to act foolish before. A time or two. Or three. "What exactly is she going to do?"

"I can hardly bear to say it aloud." Aunt Ida Belle pinched the bridge of her nose. Were those tears in her eyes? I didn't dare ask, but she was clearly upset. I'd never seen her like this. "She's fixin' to run off with the idiot," she finally said.

"What idiot?" I thought it a fair question considering this was Sinful.

"Bull Dozer," she nearly spat out his name.

"Run off as in go away for a long weekend?" Fortune asked.

Aunt Ida Belle shook her head. "No. She's leaving Sinful, and she's not coming back."

I gasped. "That can't be." When several other diners turned to look in our direction, I realized I'd spoken too loudly.

Fortune frowned. "Something's not adding up here. Why aren't you shocked, Ida Belle? Have you and Gertie spoken about this before?"

My great-aunt shook her head. "No. I put together the pieces from overhearing her talk nonsense with the pipsqueak."

The pipsqueak, I assumed, was Bull Dozer. "What do we know about him?"

Ida Belle snorted. "Nothing fit for repeating."

"We can get all the info we need," Fortune said. "It's the beauty of small town living. Where's he from originally? Sinful?"

Aunt Ida Belle shook her head. "Mudbug."

"How did Celia find out about their plans?" I asked.

"Gertie was probably flapping her gums when she went in to City Hall to pay her parking tickets." Aunt Ida Belle shook her head. "She should have known that Celia gets regular gossip reports from her minions."

Fortune nodded. "Good, getting information won't be a problem then." She turned to me. "This is as good a time as any for you to start helping us, Stephanie. But you're going to have to do things our way."

My eyes widened. What did she mean *start helping*? Hadn't I just sprinted down Main Street this morning as if I were being chased by a Malayan tiger? In the last several weeks, I'd learned that doing things their way meant being involved in shoot outs, wild car chases, meetings with mobsters, and, worst of all, regular run-ins with the newly elected mayor of Sinful.

But there'd also been plenty of laughter and a sense of camaraderie that I'd grown to cherish in a very short time. I wanted to help Gertie any way I could. "You can count on me."

"Good. We're going to need you onboard. Gertie's stubborn to begin with, add that to being under the influence of a man, and it's not a good combination."

I studied her. Fortune was a beautiful woman. Her hair was long and blond, her eyes were blue, her figure trim, but something about her story was as phony as her acrylic nails. I'd watched Fortune handle a gun like she was twirling a baton, converse with mobsters as smoothly as if she were talking to pageant judges, and I'd witnessed her take down armed opponents like she was taking off her tiara for the night. If she'd ever been a beauty queen, I'd eat my lace trimmed handkerchief.

But she'd risked her life to save mine, and for that I owed her. If she wanted to pretend to be someone she wasn't, it was fine by me. Besides, we had other things to worry about, like Gertie running off with a man she barely knew.

A funny look flitted over Fortune's face. "Carter's coming. I don't want him knowing what's going on."

Seconds later, Carter stopped by our booth. He was out of uniform, dressed in faded jeans and a plain black t-shirt that fit his well-muscled chest rather nicely, I couldn't help but notice. I glanced in Fortune's direction. Yes, she'd noticed too.

I waited for someone to say something but when no one did, I greeted him. "Hello, Carter."

"Stephanie," he nodded. "How was your trip to Hawaii?"

"Blissful," I replied, although it seemed so much longer than a week since Kase and I had arrived back in Louisiana. "If you haven't been to the islands yet, I'd highly recommend a visit."

"I'll keep that in mind. I hear Mayeux has been called back to New Orleans for a few weeks."

I nodded. "That's right. With any luck, he'll be coming back to visit on the weekends." The awkward tension in the air was palpable. "Would you care to join us?"

He shook his head. "No, thanks. Uncle Walter and I are going fishing. I just stopped by to pick up some lunch." He eyed us each in turn. "Whatever it is that y'all are up to, you'd better forget about it."

"Not that it's any of your business, young man, but we're talking about Gertie," Aunt Ida Belle said.

Fortune and I nodded in agreement. It felt good to finally be telling Deputy LeBlanc the truth for a change.

He shot a glance at the empty spot next to Fortune. "Where is she?"

"Home sick," I said.

"Car trouble," Fortune said at the exact same moment.

He frowned. "Which is it?"

"She's home, worried sick about her car trouble." It was lame but it was the best I could come up with on the spot.

"Right, like I'm going to believe that. You three are plotting some sort of nonsense. I can sense it."

Before we could demur, deny, or protest, Francine approached our booth, a pot of hot coffee in hand. "Run along now, Carter, and quit pestering these poor, innocent ladies."

I admired the way Francine could say that without cracking a smile. She'd been extra kind to me since I'd been kidnapped from the back of her restaurant. None of what happened was remotely her fault but I wasn't above accepting an extra order of fries every time we came in here. I appreciated that she was trying to run interference with Carter.

"Go on." She pointed in the direction of the kitchen. "Your packed lunches are up front. Just leave the cash by the register."

"Mind what I said," Carter warned us.

Once he'd left, we sat staring at our coffee cups. I don't know exactly what my companions were thinking, but I was struggling to envision what life in Sinful would be like without Gertie around. Unimaginable.

"We have to do something," I said. "Gertie can't go."

Aunt Ida Belle didn't look up or acknowledge my words.

Fortune stood and gathered up the take-out containers. "Let's head back to your house and hatch a game plan." She had to prod Aunt Ida Belle to get her to move. Watching my great-aunt shuffle toward the door with a downcast head was galling.

It appeared as if Swamp Team Three plus one (me) had now shrunk down to just Fortune and myself – a mismatched pair if ever there was one.

Heaven help us.

Chapter Three

BY THE TIME WE GOT back to Aunt Ida Belle's house, my feet were aching. I kicked off my shoes and slipped on a pair of pink satin bedroom slippers. The temptation to crawl back into bed and pull the covers over my head was hard to resist, but I knew Aunt Ida Belle was stewing. I made my way out to the living room. Aunt Ida Belle needed comfort. She needed company. She needed commiseration.

"You need a beer." Fortune set a bottle in front of her. "It'll help you think."

Aunt Ida Belle pushed it away. "I don't want to think."

Fortune pushed the bottle back toward her. "Then it will help you relax."

Honestly. She sounded like a snake oil saleswoman. "Herbal tea might be a better alternative." I sat beside her. "Let's remember that Gertie hasn't left yet. Maybe she's still in the planning phase, or it's just a day dream and she'll snap out of it."

"Gertie's impulsive," Fortune said.

"Impulsive and stupid are too different things," I countered.

Aunt Ida Belle punched a throw pillow. "That's just it, Gertie isn't stupid. Stubborn, yes. Clueless at times, yes. But she's never been stupid before, and especially not over a man." She threw the pillow against the far wall. "But this time something else is going on."

"Then you need to stop her." I snapped my fingers. "I know. Why don't we stage an intervention?

I saw a look pass between Aunt Ida Belle and Fortune but I couldn't decipher it. "What? Why is that a bad idea?"

"It's not that it's a bad idea," Fortune said. "It's just that Gertie's not like most people."

This much I'd figured out already.

"What Fortune means is that when Gertie gets like this, she's gonna do what she's gonna do, and there's no stopping her."

We sat in an uncomfortable silence for several torturous minutes. "I'll just put a pot of tea on then," I stood. "What do you say, Aunt Ida Belle?"

Her answer was a moan, or a groan, I'm not sure which. But I took it for a yes. I prepped the china cups, adding a plate of lady fingers to the tray. Hopefully a soothing cup of tea would work restorative wonders on her bruised heart. A few minutes later I carried the tray in and looked around the empty room. Where had they gone? "Fortune?" I called out. There was no answer. "Aunt Ida Belle?"

I blew out a long, and I'll admit, exasperated breath. These women were wonderful human beings but absolutely unlike any other women I'd ever known. Spending time with them was akin to socializing on an alien planet. I set the tea tray on the coffee table. My great-aunt's beer sat untouched. I didn't see Fortune's bottle so she couldn't have gone far.

She hadn't.

I found her sitting on the front steps. "May I?"

She waved her hand at the empty space beside her. "Be my guest."

I sat and arranged my skirt to cover my knees. "I thought maybe you and Aunt Ida Belle had taken off after Gertie."

Fortune shook her head. "I suggested that very thing but Ida Belle said she wanted to take a nap."

"Oh." I hardly knew what to say to that. My aunt wasn't the napping kind.

"Exactly. That tells you how bad this is." She took a long swig of beer. "I've never seen Gertie acting this crazy before either."

"What do you suggest we do?" I had no ideas of my own.

She shifted so that she sat facing me. "I'm glad you asked. I propose we team up and get to the bottom of this."

"What if this is what Gertie really wants? What if it's what makes her happy? I'm not sure it's our place to stand between her and happiness."

"I'm not saying that we keep her from dating Bull if that's what she wants," Fortune said. "But she needs to slow down this runaway train. Leaving town is extreme, especially since she's just met this guy."

I decided to play devil's advocate. "Sometimes it doesn't take long to decide you're really attracted to someone. How long did it take you and Carter to recognize there was something between you?"

"Twice the time it took you and Agent Mayeux," she shot back. "Look, I'm not good at this kind of touchy-feely girl talk. No one wants Gertie to be unhappy. It's just that we don't think she should run off and start a new life without thinking it through."

It suddenly occurred to me that I had no idea where Gertie and Bull were headed. "All this fuss isn't because she's moving to Mudbug, is it?"

"Try Los Angeles."

My eyes widened. Gertie in Los Angeles? Oh, dear.

"Exactly. It's a bit of an extreme move, isn't it?"

From the Louisiana bayou to the City of Angels? I nodded. "It definitely is."

"I know you haven't been here long, Stephanie, and I haven't either for that matter. But I do know your aunt and she would never stand in the way of what was good for Gertie. Even if it meant Gertie leaving town. Ida Belle's a smart woman and she's known Gertie her whole life. If she feels that this is wrong, it likely is."

I took her point. "If I've figured out anything since I've arrived, it's that Gertie and Ida Belle are true friends," I said. I'd also figured out that Fortune wasn't exactly who she said she was, but I knew Aunt Ida Belle trusted her implicitly. That held sway with me. But what did she see in Fortune that I didn't? Maybe working with her to sort out this Gertie thing would help me get to know the real Fortune. "Okay, I'm in. I'll help however I can."

"Good." Fortune stood and extended a hand. I got to my feet and we shook hands, a new alliance formed through our mutual caring for Aunt Ida Belle and Gertie.

I felt a surge of certainty that with a bit of delicate handling, we could bring some sanity to the situation. "How do you suggest we start?"

"With breaking and entering."

Of course. Why didn't I see that coming?

WE ARRIVED IN MUDBUG just about the time my stomach started to growl. "Is there any place to eat here?" I looked around as Fortune guided her Jeep down the town's main street. "Do they have the equivalent of Francine's Diner here?"

"Don't they wish." Fortune swung into a parking space. "There's a place called Spanky's down at the end of this street. My guess is that they'll know of Bull in there."

My eyebrow's rose. "Spanky's?" If she thought I was going to hang out in a strip joint, on a Sunday no less, she was crazy. I told her so.

"Spanky's isn't a strip club. It's a diner. The owner is a cantankerous old guy named Spanky, but he won't be there today. He takes Sundays off."

"How do you know all of this?" I asked.

She shrugged. "Recon comes naturally to me."

I decided not to ask. If she and I were going to be successful in working together, I was going to have to let some things slide.

"My source told me—"

Make that a lot of things.

"—that Gertie and Bull were heading in to New Orleans for the day," Fortune continued. "That gives us plenty of time to do what we came to do."

"Which is?"

"You're heading to Spanky's to grab a bite to eat. While you're there, discreetly ask about Bull. See what you can find out. Just leave Gertie's name out of it. Can you handle that?"

"Of course," I lied. "I'll just sashay in there, make up a story out of thin air, and start gathering information. Piece of cake." Unfortunately, my words came out a bit more sarcastic than I meant for them to. I really needed to do better if we were going to work together. "What about breaking and entering? When are we doing that part?"

"We're not. I am." Her expression was slightly apologetic. "No offense, but you'll slow me down. Besides, you're not dressed for it." She gave my kitten heeled sandals a pointed look. "Not very practical if we need to do some running."

I looked down. She was right. I'd chosen these sandals because they were white and it was almost September. Labor Day would be upon us soon and I'd have to put them away until after Memorial Day. "You don't need a look-out?"

She shook her head. "No. I'm heading over to the boarding house where Bull has a room. You'd look conspicuous standing around in your Sunday finest."

And so it was settled. Fortune drove off, promising to be back within the hour. I headed for Spanky's, determined to uncover information to share with Fortune.

THE TIME THAT I SPENT at Spanky's hole in the wall, for I wouldn't call it a diner, was the longest twenty minutes of my life. From the moment I pushed open the door and stepped in, I felt more out of place than I could ever remember feeling before. One quick look around the darkened interior was all I needed to see to know that I'd much rather have been breaking into Bull's lodging. Still, however uncomfortable I was, I had a job to do.

I perched on a barstool at the counter. The bar top was sticky, so I kept my hands in my lap. The establishment was more than half full, and the clientele predominantly male. I didn't have to wait long before the bartender made his way over to me.

"Well, lookee here, ain't you prim and proper?"

My eyebrows rose. "You know who I am?"

His forehead wrinkled into a frown. "Huh?"

My cheeks flamed as I realized that he didn't recognize me, he was mocking me. "I'd like a lemonade please."

In short order he set a glass of something yellow in front of me. There was no way I was willing to add my fingerprints to the several dozen that adorned the glass, however, so I didn't reach for it. My mind raced to think of a way to get the information I'd come for so I could get out of there. "I was hoping you could help me," I said to the bartender. "I'm looking for a Mr. Dozer."

He wiped the counter but didn't raise his eyes to meet mine. "Bull?"

"Yes, that's right. Do you know him?" I waited for an answer but none came so I plunged ahead. "I recently attended a wedding where things got a bit out of hand." A true understatement considering the amount of blood that had been shed. "Mr. Dozer was kind enough to assist us in keeping order. I wanted to thank him."

"Why didn't you thank him then?"

How to answer this? Because the bride's father had been shot dead minutes before the ceremony, and three people, including my great-aunt had been kidnapped, and we went chasing after them. There was just no way to make that sound coherent. "Things got hectic, I'm afraid. Would you be so kind as to tell me where he's employed so I can drop by tomorrow and thank him in person?"

The bartender threw back his head and laughed. A few of the other patrons at the bar snickered. "Bull, work?" He shook his head. "You must have the wrong guy. His full-time job is to avoid work."

"Oh." That certainly took the wind out of my sails. It had never occurred to me that Bull was retired. I didn't know his precise age but he didn't look much over fifty, fifty-five tops. Had Gertie mentioned something about his line of work? I strained to remember but I couldn't come up with anything definitive.

Embarrassing as it was, I had to admit that when Gertie began to gush about Bull, I hadn't listened as carefully as I might have.

I thanked the bartender, laid a five-dollar bill next to my untouched lemonade, and hurried out into the sunshine to wait for Fortune. Hopefully, she'd been more successful than I had, which shouldn't be difficult considering that I'd come up with exactly nothing.

I knew I was early and would have time to kill before Fortune returned for me, but only a few moments after I'd reached our designated meeting spot, I heard her Jeep careen around a corner. With eyes wide, I watched as she came to a screeching stop in front of me.

"Get in," she ordered.

I used both hands to wave away the dust she'd kicked up by tearing down the street like that. "What on earth is going on?"

"Just get a move on," she barked, glancing over her shoulder. "We don't have time to lollygag."

Her words propelled me into action. I rushed around to the passenger seat and jumped in. My bum was barely in the seat before she gunned the engine and we tore off. I fumbled for my seat belt and clicked it into place before I shifted in my seat to face her. "Good heavens, Fortune, why are you driving like the devil's chasing us?"

She ignored my question for a good half of the trip. I held my tongue until she dropped her speed to a mere twenty miles over the speed limit. "Did you find out anything?" I asked.

She glanced over at me and nodded. "Bull's trouble."

This didn't entirely surprise me. "How much trouble?"

"Plenty," she replied. "I think he's planning to kill Gertie."

Chapter Four

NEITHER OF US SPOKE for the remainder of the drive back to Sinful. Half-formed questions swirled through my mind as I struggled to make sense of her words. What could she possibly have found in Bull's room that would lead her to the conclusion that his intentions towards Gertie were nefarious?

The one thing that wasn't going through my mind was that Fortune was being either histrionic or delusional. Admittedly, in the past, I've had reservations about her grasp on reality. Gertie had sworn me to secrecy a few weeks back and told me that Fortune was a CIA Agent who was hiding out in Sinful because an arms dealer had a price on her head. Naturally, I'd summarily dismissed this as nonsense, a prank that Gertie was playing on the new girl in town, namely me, to test how gullible I was. I'd even gone so far as to ask Ally about the rumor, but she'd laughed the notion off as silly.

But was it? I glanced over at Fortune's profile. There was so much about her that didn't make sense to me, but here's what I did know. She was smart, strong, skilled in hand-to-hand combat, and her story about being in Sinful to settle an estate had as many holes in it as a common kitchen strainer. However, my great-aunt Ida Belle trusted Fortune implicitly, and I'd been in town long enough to know that this wasn't an honor she bestowed on many people.

And then there was my new beau. I had enormous respect for Kase's judgement. Aside from being sexy in bad-boy sort of way, he was intelligent, astute, and an FBI Agent himself. My gut instinct told me that he believed Fortune was something other than what she said she was, although he'd never said so directly. It made sense that Kase would be able to identify a federal fellow agent. I snuck a covert peek at her profile. Could it be true? Was she an undercover agent?

"Why do you keep looking at me like that?" Fortune asked, her eyes never leaving the road in front of us.

"You're not a librarian, are you?"

"Not at the moment, no."

Nice dodge but I wasn't giving up that easily. "I'm on to you, Fortune. Both Kase and Gertie have already told me what you really do for a living." Technically that was a bit of a fudge because Kase hadn't verbalized any such thing, but I needed what Gertie would call 'verbal dynamite' to get this conversation up to full speed. "It's time to fess up."

Fortune laughed. "Gee, Stephanie, how could I ever stand up to interrogation like that?"

"So, it's true?"

She shook her head but kept her eyes on the road in front of her. When it became obvious that she wasn't going to say anything, I ploughed ahead. "You leave me with little choice. I'm going to have to ask Aunt Ida Belle for the truth. She won't lie to me."

I watched as Fortune bit her lip. Ah, ha. I *was* on to something.

"Maybe she would lie if she were protecting a friend, hypothetically speaking, of course. Your aunt is one of the most loyal people I've ever met," Fortune said. "Why put her in that position?"

"I could ask you the same thing," I retorted. "Why not just tell me the truth so she doesn't have to choose between us?"

Instead of answering, Fortune guided the Jeep to the shoulder of the road. She came to a stop, cut the engine, and looked at me for a long moment before she spoke. "If you've already figured things out, why would you need it confirmed?"

I sensed this was as close an admission as I was ever going to receive. "I never did buy that you were a beauty queen, Fortune. Not that you're not beautiful, but you just didn't sell it."

She lifted an eyebrow. "I'll take that as a compliment. Now, what do you plan on doing with the information you think you have on me?"

I touched my pearl necklace. "Why nothing, of course. Your secret is safe with me."

She closed her eyes and muttered under her breath as she started up the Jeep and headed back onto the road. "My life depends on you keeping your trap shut."

So eloquently put. But I took her point. "I won't say another word about this, not to you, or anyone else. I promise."

She nodded. "Thank you. Now, let's direct our attention back to where it belongs. Gertie needs our help."

We both remained lost in our own thoughts for the remainder of the trip back to Sinful. I don't know what luck Fortune was having making sense of all of this but I was lost in a fog of confusion. My only hope was that Aunt Ida Belle would meet us when we pulled up at her front door with the news that she'd figured out a solution to the trouble that Gertie was courting.

But as Fortune turned onto Aunt Ida Belle's street, I realized this wasn't going to happen. An ambulance with flashing lights was parked in front of my great-aunt's house. Carter's pick-up truck was just behind it.

Fortune and I exchanged worried glances.

The trouble, it seemed, was just beginning.

"IF THEY POKE ME ONE more time, I'm going to raise holy hell."

From the chair next to her hospital bedside, I reached out and patted my great-aunt's arm. The one that wasn't broken. I didn't blame her for being downright ornery but she wasn't in a position to raise her head off the pillow, let alone raise a ruckus. "They're just trying to help you." I strove to keep my voice as soothing as possible. "You took quite a tumble, and for someone of your age—"

Her growl warned me that I'd taken a verbal misstep. I glanced at Fortune, who stood by the window.

"Buck up, Ida Belle," she said. "You had a bit of bad luck and now you're going to have to tough it out."

This rather rough and tumble approach seemed to soothe my great-aunt. She nodded. "I know. I feel so stupid."

"Don't," Fortune and I said at precisely the same time.

"Well, I do." Aunt Ida Belle winced as she tried to shift in the bed. "Have you been able to track down Gertie?"

I shook my head. "Not yet, I'm afraid. But I know she'll come here as soon as she checks her messages."

Aunt Ida Belle grunted in response. Doubtless, we were all thinking the same thing. Gertie was off somewhere with Bull. Who knew when she'd check in?

"Maybe it's better we have a chance to talk without her," Fortune said. She pulled a chair next to the other side of the bed. "There's something I need to tell you both."

I nodded, eager to hear a follow-up to her earlier bombshell. "We're listening."

"Bull's room was a pig-sty as far as his clothes and whatnot went," she said. "But his personal papers were neatly filed in a firebox." She leaned forward, her brow knit in a worried frown.

"That frown of yours tells me you found something," Aunt Ida Belle said. "Just spit it out already."

"Bull's taken out a life insurance policy on Gertie."

I gasped. "That's not good."

Fortune met my eye. "No, it's not."

"The rat bastard." Aunt Ida Belle struggled to sit up but Fortune and I both held out a restraining arm so that she couldn't. "I'm going to kill him."

Fortune nodded approvingly. "Fine by me, but considering your broken arm, you're going to need some help."

"We can't kill him," I protested. I looked to Fortune for guidance. "Can we?"

"Of course we can, but we probably shouldn't," she conceded, sounding more than a little disappointed. "But that doesn't mean we can't find a way to nail his nasty little ass to the wall."

"Preferably a prison wall," Aunt Ida Belle chimed in.

Before I could respond, a nurse bustled into the room. "Am I interrupting something?" she asked, her voice cheerful.

"We're in the middle of plotting a murder." Aunt Ida Belle motioned toward the door with her good arm. "Get out."

The nurse's shocked expression propelled me to my feet. I laid a hand on her shoulder. "Don't worry, she's exaggerating. We're not planning an actual murder. Just a takedown, of sorts." I gently propelled her in the direction of the door. "We're not quite through. Would it be possible for you to return in half an hour, let's say?"

With one last uncertain glance at each of us, she nodded and left.

"You've got to help spring me," Aunt Ida Belle implored, looking between us. "I can't stay here."

"I doubt Medicaid would let you even if you wanted to," Fortune said. "But you can't go home either."

"Why not?" I asked. I hardly considered that Fortune's call to make. "I'm perfectly able and willing to take care of her."

"I don't need a damn nursemaid." Aunt Ida Belle's frown could easily be classified as a category five storm. She attempted to reach the call button but couldn't manage. "Stephanie, get a nurse in here. I want my discharge papers, pronto."

Fortune shook her head. "Not so fast. No one's going anywhere until we hatch a plan."

I bit back the annoyed retort that sprang to my lips. I was going to make every effort to get along with Fortune, even if it killed me. I stayed where I was, ignoring Aunt Ida Belle's request that I chase after the nurse she'd just exiled a moment before.

"Oh, I've got a plan, don't you fret. I'm going to get out of this bed, track down that piece of slime, tar and feather him, and then set Gertie straight. Stephanie, get me my clothes."

I sat back and folded my hands neatly in my lap. "I'll do no such thing while you're spouting nonsense, Aunt Ida Belle."

She shot me a nasty look and then turned her attention to Fortune. "You've got to help me."

Fortune shook her head. "You've got that backwards, Ida Belle. You're the one who's going to help us."

My great-aunt and I exchanged confused looks.

"She is?"

"I am?"

"You are," Fortune confirmed. "By going undercover."

I closed my eyes rather than roll them. Honestly, these women seemed to think life was one long Starsky and Hutch episode.

"Wake up, kid," Aunt Ida Belle said. "It sounds like things are just about to get interesting. You don't want to miss this."

Au contraire. I very much did want to miss out on whatever was coming next. But I opened my eyes and looked at Fortune. "What do you have planned?"

"I think it's best if Ida Belle checks into a nursing home for a few weeks to recuperate from her broken arm."

"Like hell I will," Aunt Ida Belle shot back. "I'm going home."

"Why would she go into a nursing home if I'm able to care for her at home?" I asked.

"Because when I was going through Bull's papers, I happened to notice that he is the co-owner of a nursing home in Sinful."

"Which one?" Aunt Ida Belle demanded. "There aren't that many around these parts."

"Bayou Gardens, out by the casino."

"That swamp hole? Nonsense." Aunt Ida Belle waved her good hand dismissively. "The Lisieux family has owned that dump since before the Korean War broke out."

Fortune shrugged. "Well, it appears they've recently taken on a new partner."

I cocked my head to the side and thought. Bull the business owner? That didn't match up with what I'd heard earlier at Spanky's. I said so.

"More proof he's shady," Fortune said. "Look, maybe this whole silent partner thing is legitimate and he just doesn't want to blow his cover as a professional lazy-ass. But there's no reason that he needs to have an insurance policy on Gertie's life."

"Not unless he plans on taking it," Aunt Ida Belle said.

"So, you're willing to let Stephanie check you into the Lisieux's place? Just long enough for us to get some dirt on Bull?" Fortune asked.

Aunt Ida Belle didn't hesitate. "Of course, I will. But don't let me be catching sight of that runt out there or I won't be responsible for my actions." She flexed her good hand. "I only need one arm to take him out."

Fortune and I exchanged knowing glances. Bull Dozer could easily go from being the hunter to the hunted if Aunt Ida Belle had her way.

"Knock, knock." Gertie's chipper voice broke through the strained silence. She pushed open the door and stuck her head in. "You started the party without me?"

How exactly to respond to her levity in the face of what we feared, I didn't know, so I remained silent.

Aunt Ida Belle didn't share my hesitation. "Where the hell have you been?"

Gertie slipped in the room and stood at the end of the bed, her expression sheepish. "On a picnic. I forgot my cell phone in Bull's truck, but Carter tracked us down." Her eyes traveled over the cast that ran from my great-aunt's wrist, straight up her arm past her elbow. "Bull was such a sweetheart, you should have seen how concerned he was. He drove me straight over here."

I shivered, which had nothing to do with the fact that air conditioner was cranked up. None of this made any sense, but the ache in the pit of my stomach confirmed that I agreed with Fortune's assessment of the situation.

Bull Dozer wanted Gertie dead.

And it was up to us to stop him.

Chapter Five

"I DON'T LIKE THIS, darlin', not one bit."

The concern in my boyfriend's voice made me want to purr like my prize Persian cat did when she was feeling especially content. Kase Mayeux had that effect on me, but the worry laced in his words wasn't lost on me either. "I'll be fine, Kase. Fortune will be with me."

He groaned. "I'm not sure if that makes me feel better or worse."

I glanced across the parking lot at Fortune, who stood talking to Carter. Something about her body language made me think she was doing much the same as I was, namely trying to avoid outright lies as we downplayed what we were up to. I appreciated that Kase worried about my safety. The very last thing I wanted to do was be dishonest with him, at least any more than I had to, because we were such a new couple. "I miss you," I said. Heaven knew that was the truth.

"I miss you too, darlin'." He was silent for a long moment. "Can't any of this wait until I can get down there this weekend?"

"No. We need to move fast. Who knows what that odious little man has planned?" I still couldn't believe this was happening. It was like something out of a bad dream. "Maybe we'll have Gertie seeing straight before you arrive on Friday."

"Hope so." But he sounded like he doubted it as much as I did.

I said a quick goodbye when I saw Fortune heading my way. Carter waved as he drove past but the grim set of his face didn't escape my notice. Once we were in the Jeep and on our way out to visit Bayou Gardens, I asked Fortune just how much she'd told him.

"Not much," she admitted. "We're, well, our relationship is complicated."

"How so?" I asked.

For several minutes she didn't say anything, she just kept her eyes on the road in front of us. "You're not going to let this go either, are you?"

I shook my head. "No, I'm not. It's past time we get to know each other better. Share confidences. Girlfriend stuff, you know?"

Her frown might well have offended someone with less confidence than I possessed but I wasn't about to be deterred. "Did you tell Carter about Bull possibly being involved with Bayou Gardens? Or about the life insurance policy?"

"No and no." She glanced over at me. "I'm guessing you spilled everything to Kase."

I gave a noncommittal shrug. I hardly considered sharing ninety percent of what I knew with my boyfriend as 'spilling everything'. "I conveyed the pertinent information."

"Yeah, well, enough chatting about clues, Miss Marple. The less people who know about this the better. In a town this size you can't afford to tell anyone anything, unless you want everyone in town to know about it within hours. Talk spreads like wildfire."

Paranoid much? I left the words unsaid, however. Perhaps it was a part of her training to be so inherently distrustful. "I'll be discreet."

She nodded. "I did tell Carter that we were going to check out the nursing home, and I asked him to check out their complaint record with the state board. But he thinks I'm asking as a concerned friend. Let's leave it at that."

We drove on in silence. I marveled at the way the terrain gave away to swampland as Sinful fell behind us. Who would have thought of building a retirement center way out in the middle of nowhere? "Do you know anything about the Lisieux family?"

She shook her head. "Nothing. You?"

"I don't believe I've heard anyone mention them, but then, I haven't been in town very long."

"Sometimes that works for us, sometimes against us," Fortune said. "Some folks think because we're Yankees we're too clueless to understand what they're saying so they'll natter on. Others clam up." She slowed the Jeep as we drove down a rutted dirt road overgrown with low hanging cypress trees. "Let's hope whoever shows us around is in a chatty mood."

They weren't.

"So what sort of leisure activities do you offer?" I asked Ramona, the woman who was showing us around. Her expression was dour, her mouth appeared to be drooped into a perpetual tight line, and she made a point of looking everywhere but at me when I spoke. But I soldiered on. "You know, things like square dancing or ceramics?"

"I thought your aunt had a broken arm? Why would she want to square dance?"

Why indeed? I glanced back over my shoulder to see if Fortune was still with us. She was in sight but dragging along slowly enough that she didn't have to participate in the conversation. Lucky her. I'd have an easier time conversing with the giraffes at the Boston Zoo than this woman. "You're right, of course. What my great-aunt needs is to have a quiet place to heal."

Ramona shrugged. "Okay, fine, we're as good a place as any to sit and recuperate."

More like sit and watch the paint dry, if the glazed look on the faces of the other residents we'd glanced earlier were any indication. Aunt Ida Belle was going to hate it here. I almost felt sorry for the staff. They had no idea what they were in for. "Well, Ramona, I need to be very upfront with you. My great-aunt is a feisty sort by nature. Her incapacitation has only made her more—challenging, shall we say?"

"Are you saying she's a pain in the ass?"

I gasped. "No, of course not."

"Because we can give her something for that. Something to take the edge off." She hugged her clipboard to her chest and looked at me with uninterested eyes. "Do you want a room or not?"

I swallowed hard. "Yes, we do." I experienced a stab of guilt as I spoke. Essentially, I was sacrificing my great-aunt to save Gertie. Truly, an untenable situation if ever there was one.

Ramona thrust her clipboard at me. "Here are the monthly costs of being a Bayou Gardens resident."

I glanced at the numbers and then back at Ramona. "Those numbers are per *month*?"

She studied me. "Yes, per month. Is that a problem?"

"No, of course not," I hurried to assure her. No price was too high to pay to save Gertie's life. Although for the cost of a month's stay at Bayou Gardens, I could send Aunt Ida Belle on a cruise of the Greek Isles and still have money left over to refurbish the Parthenon. "Am I to assume that this figure includes a private room?"

Ramona shook her head. "No. No one here has a private room. We're nearly full to capacity."

I glanced up and down the empty corridor. A more lifeless place, I could hardly imagine. Aunt Ida Belle was going to have my head on a platter for sticking her here. Heaven help us all.

"The security deposit is a full month's rent due at signing, along with the first month's rent." She pulled a pen from her skirt pocket and held it out to me. "Management prefers cash."

Fortune's arrival saved me from my spluttering. She took the clipboard from me, slipped the papers out of it, and handed it back to Ramona. "We'll be back tomorrow to finalize things." She propelled me toward the front door. "Have to run, we've got a family emergency," she called back over her shoulder.

As we burst out of Bayou Gardens, she gave me a gentle shove toward her Jeep. "Hurry up and get in."

I did as she bid, not at all certain she'd wait for me if I didn't. I clicked my seat belt into place as she peeled out of the parking lot. "Isn't this all bit of overkill?" I asked. "I mean, I didn't like it in there any more than you did but—"

"Gertie's been hurt," she interrupted me. "Carter just texted me."

A wave of dread washed over me. "Hurt how?"

She glanced at me, her expression skeptical. "Allegedly, she fell and hit her head."

"Allegedly," I repeated. "You think Bull hurt her?"

She nodded. "I know he did."

"It couldn't have been an accident?" I asked, hoping against hope.

She gripped the steering wheel so tight her knuckles turned white. "Accident my ass."

While that was hardly language I'd have chosen, we both knew she was right. Bull had made his first attempt to kill Gertie.

WE MET CARTER IN THE hallway outside of Gertie's hospital room.

"How is she?" Fortune asked before I could. "Wait, she isn't alone in there, is she?"

Carter shook his head. "No. A nurse is in with her." He glanced at his watch. "You two made it back here in record time. Doubt you could have done that by driving the speed limit."

Fortune shrugged. "We were worried."

"Has Bull been in to see her?" I asked.

"No, I don't think so," Carter answered. "I haven't seen him since he dropped Gertie off a couple of hours ago. I don't know if he's still hanging around."

Oh, he was, I had no doubt.

"How bad is her head injury?" Fortune asked. "Can we see her?"

"From what I understand, she got lucky. If she'd fallen an inch to the right, according to the doctor, she'd have hit her temple and done some serious damage." He shook his head. "It's rare to see both Gertie and Ida Belle down and out."

Fortune and I exchanged a quick look. Better Gertie be down and out rather than six feet under.

"Where did Gertie fall?" I asked. "Was she alone?"

He nodded. "She was visiting with Ida Belle until your aunt needed to go down to radiology. A short while later, a nurse found her on the floor." He leaned in and kissed Fortune's cheek. "I'm going to take off now that you too are here. Let me know if Gertie needs anything."

Fortune reached out and tugged on his sleeve as he moved away. "Did you happen to learn anything about Bayou Gardens while we were gone?"

"Yeah, I had Myrtle look into it. According to her, there's been a ton of complaints filed about the food, the lack of air conditioning, and things of that nature. Nothing the state finds actionable though." He looked between us both. "Any particular reason that you're not taking Ida Belle home to recover? She's not exactly the nursing home type."

"You're right, she's not." I said, "But I might have to go to Boston next week and I want to make sure she'll be looked after."

Carter's expression was skeptical. "Why doesn't she come stay with you, Fortune?"

When she didn't answer right away, I jumped in. "Fortune might be coming with me. To a White Glove Convention."

Carter's eyebrows shot up but we were saved from further questioning by his cell phone. He glanced at the caller id, told us that it was urgent, and took off at a jog down the corridor.

Once he was out of sight, Fortune threw up her hands. "Really, Stephanie? A White Glove Convention? I don't even know what that is, but Carter's smart enough to know that it's no place I'm likely to be."

"Honestly, Fortune, I don't know what you want from me. When you didn't answer, I jumped in to help you. After all, we're partners now."

"If you two are done bickering now, we can go in and see Gertie."

We whirled around in unison to find Aunt Ida Belle standing in front of Gertie's door. "Oh, Aunt Ida Belle, I didn't hear you approach. Why aren't you in a wheelchair?"

She made a face that looked like she'd just drank curdled milk. "My legs aren't broken, my arm is." She jerked her head in the direction of Gertie's door. "We got lucky this time but we can't afford to lose focus. Now, let's get in there and find out what Gertie remembers."

"Wait, there's a nurse in there," I told her.

"We'll make short work of her," she assured me, in a tone that was decidedly cantankerous.

She pushed open the door and hastened to do just that. Not a full minute later, a nurse charged out of Gertie's room and headed down toward the nurse's station, all the while mumbling under her breath. We slipped in the room.

Gertie lay back against the pillows, her head bandaged, but she was awake and her smile was bright. I experienced a wave of affection mingled with relief. I sat in the chair beside her, while Fortune sat at the foot of the bed.

"You scared us, Gertie." I covered her hand with mine. "How are you feeling?"

Her lips lifted in a half smile, half grimace. "I don't remember. One minute I was standing there talking to myself, and the next minute, I was on the floor."

"You were trying to show me up," Aunt Ida Belle said from her chair by the window. "You just couldn't let me have my fall without trying to one up me, could you?"

Gertie grinned. "At least I didn't break anything."

My great-aunt harrumphed. "That's because your head is hard as a rock."

This good-natured banter between them, full of genuine affection, was proof that Gertie and Aunt Ida Belle were the best of friends. Listening to them softened my heart, but also hardened my resolve to eliminate Bull Dozer from the picture. "Were you alone when you fell?" I asked.

Gertie nodded.

"Bull wasn't with you?" Fortune asked.

"No." She shifted, clearly uncomfortable. "He dropped me off after Carter told us that Ida Belle had been hurt. I was in here alone waiting for her to come back when I fell. Why?"

"Hold up," Aunt Ida Belle said. "Didn't he bring you a fancy-schmancy coffee latte thing just before I left?"

Gertie's face brightened. "That's right. I forgot. What a sweetheart. Maybe I should see if he's got a friend for you, Ida Belle. We could double date."

A quick glance at my great-aunt confirmed what I thought. She was about to blow louder than the noon whistle.

"I doubt Walter would appreciate that," I said.

"Where's your coffee cup?" Fortune got to her feet and began to look around the room. "Were you holding it when you fell?"

Gertie shrugged. "I don't know. I can't remember. Why?" She looked between us. "What's going on? You're all acting strange."

I stood and straightened her blanket. "We're worried about you, Gertie. It's been quite a day. Would you like me to fluff your pillows?" When she nodded, I did so, making sure to keep up a stream of chatter to give Fortune time to search for the coffee cup. But she didn't find one, and soon excused herself from the room. I imagined she was going to talk to someone in housekeeping but I doubted Bull had left any evidence lying around.

"When can we go home?" Gertie's words were followed by a yawn. "I want to sleep in my own bed."

I pulled the blanket up and tucked it around her shoulders as her eyelids grew heavy. "We'll wait to see what the doctor says when she comes in." I turned to Aunt Ida Belle. "You should go get some rest too. I'll stay here with Gertie."

Reluctantly, she got to her feet. "I hate to admit it, but I could use a few winks. Just promise that you'll stay here until Fortune comes to spell you."

"You have my word." I opened the door for her but jumped back in surprise when I saw Bull standing just in the doorway. "Oh, mercy."

He grinned. "Didn't mean to startle you."

I quickly stepped in front of Aunt Ida Belle as she advanced toward Bull. "Gertie's just drifted off. Let's you and I have a little talk in the corridor."

Once the door to her room closed behind us, I stood in front of it. Bull wasn't getting anywhere near Gertie on my watch. I linked my arm through Aunt Ida Belle's good arm.

"How's my Gertie-girl?" he asked, with a grin that would have better suited a leprechaun than a grown man.

"Don't call her that," Aunt Ida Belle snapped.

Bull's jaw tightened. "She's okay, though, right?"

"Gertie will be fine," I assured him. The sooner he went away the better. Even with only one working arm, I knew Aunt Ida Belle could hog-tie him in seconds flat. "We'll take excellent care of her, don't you worry." When he didn't respond, I added, "I'll call you tomorrow morning with an update."

"Morning?" He shook his head and made a tsking sound. "I can't be without my girl that long. I'm here to take her home."

I tightened my hold on my great-aunt's arm and forced myself to smile. "No need for you to go to the trouble when we're heading that way anyhow." I forced myself to smile. "Gertie will understand if you need to head back to work. I'm sure she won't want you missing too many hours on her account."

He opened his mouth to protest but Fortune and the attending doctor joined us. I made the introductions and then asked the doctor about Gertie's release.

"She'll need watching," the doctor warned us.

"Doesn't she always?" Aunt Ida Belle muttered under her breath.

Fortune smiled, Bull frowned, and the doctor raised an eyebrow. "Pardon?"

"Just an inside family joke," I assured her. "We'll provide Gertie with around the clock care."

"Excellent." She consulted Gertie's chart. "The tests don't give us any indication that your friend had a seizure or stroke. She avoided a serious injury this time but she may not be so lucky next time. Until we know why she fell, someone needs to be with her constantly in case she gets dizzy again."

"We will, no worries there." I shook the doctor's hand. "I know she'll be happy that she can go home."

Aunt Ida Belle shook her head. "She's not going home."

"She's not?" Bull and I asked simultaneously.

"Nope. She's going to be staying at the old folk's home with me."

"What old folk's home?" Bull demanded.

Aunt Ida Belle met his gaze straight on. "Bayou Gardens."

Bull's face flushed red. "Ah, hell no. I can't have my girl in a place like that." He crossed his arms over his chest. "Over my dead body."

Chapter Six

FORTUNATELY FOR BULL, it didn't come to that. Not only was he alive, he was swarming around us like a fly at a picnic as we settled Gertie into her room at Bayou Gardens. Talking her into staying had been no easy task. However, after far too much back and forth, Fortune and I agreed to play the Ida Belle card. Our call turned out to be a good one too, because as soon as we led Gertie to water, she drank.

"Oh, I hadn't thought of that," she said, as she looked between us. She nodded sagely. "But you're right. Ida Belle would be embarrassed at the idea of moving into an old folk's home."

Fortune, who sat at the end of Gertie's bed, quickly agreed. "You know how people talk. She'd hate what they would say about her being old and infirm."

I felt guilty for misleading Gertie but it was for her own good. Wasn't it? I glanced at Fortune. What if she'd been wrong about Bull? What if what she thought she'd seen in his room hadn't been a life insurance policy but something else? Something innocent?

She met my gaze and I was struck by the worry in her eyes. Suddenly, my doubts vaporized. Whatever threat Fortune perceived, it was real. "I'll run home and get some things for you, Gertie. Carter said he'd keep an eye on your place, so there's nothing for you to worry about."

"I've got a couple of casseroles in the fridge that need to be eaten."

Fortune waved away her concern. "We'll eat some and take the rest to Marie's house. If I'm not mistaken, it's her turn to host bridge tomorrow night." She got to her feet. "Looks like we're all set. I'll help you get dressed and you can sign your discharge papers while Stephanie gathers your things."

Gertie nodded thoughtfully but stayed uncharacteristically silent.

"What is it?" I asked. Doubtless she was tired, and I imagined her heart hurt, but something else was clearly troubling her. Maybe she was having doubts about her choice in boyfriends. Better yet, maybe she'd remembered something about Bull that was incriminating. "Tell us what's got you looking so worried."

She clutched the blanket to her chest in a move that made her appear vulnerable. "This isn't it, is it? I mean, Ida Belle and I aren't going to spend forever sitting in rocking chairs at Bayou Gardens, are we?" Her eyes watered. "I thought we had decades yet before that would happen."

I leaned in and hugged her. "Of course not. It's only temporary while Aunt Ida Belle's arm heals. I promise."

Fortune laid a gentle hand on Gertie's shoulder. "Don't be crazy, Gertie. What would Sinful be like without you and Ida Belle keeping everyone in check? Oh, Lord, think of what havoc Celia would wreck if she thought you two were out of the picture. Yeah, not gonna happen."

Gertie grinned. "Okay, let's do this."

Less than three hours later, both Aunt Ida Belle and Gertie were checked into Bayou Gardens. The place was not aptly named. Well, perhaps the bayou part. Heaven knew it smelled swampy enough. But the gardens? Hardly apropos unless the landscape architect was going for a jungle themed look, which I doubted. The place was just flat out run down and overrun with foliage.

I plopped into a plastic chair just outside of the entrance. "I'm exhausted."

Fortune sat beside me. "It's been a hell of a day, I'll give you that. No offense, but your aunt is a pain in the ass when she's mad."

"I think that's part of her charm."

We laughed, which felt good because the gawd-awful worry about Gertie's safety weighed heavily on us both. "Do you think we're doing the right thing? What if Gertie being here only puts her more directly in the line of fire?"

"That's a risk we're taking, yes. But she's safest if she's being watched every moment. Ida Belle can do that here while we focus on Bull."

The idea of focusing on Bull turned my stomach. "Why can't we just kidnap him and torture the truth out of him?"

"Don't think I'm not tempted but there's a little thing called the law standing in our way." She slapped her hands on her knees and stood. "Let's get to work."

I stood but I literally didn't know which direction to turn. "Are we going back in or heading somewhere else?" If there was a game plan, I hadn't seen it.

"You're going in as my cover." She stretched and flexed. "What I need you to do is be your most annoying self—" she broke off when I raised an eyebrow "—sorry, I meant your most prim and proper self to create a distraction with the front desk staff and the manager while I nose around the property."

I decided to ignore her inaccurate assessment of my disposition. After all, it had been a long day and we were a team now, however mismatched. "Wouldn't it be better if I stayed with Gertie?"

She shook her head. "Ida Belle's on it. Trust me, she needs something to do or she'll jump out of her skin. She knows not to let Gertie take a single pill or eat a bite of food unless we provide it."

I nodded. To anyone else the idea might sound ludicrous, but I knew that even with only one functioning arm, Aunt Ida Belle could keep trouble at bay. What I felt less sure about was what Fortune and I were going to do on our part to nail Bull.

Fortune pointed to the entrance. "It's show time, Stephanie."

"I'M TELLING YOU IT was a RAT." I threw my arms wide and didn't try to modulate my faux-panicked tone. After all, panic was a perfectly legitimate response in the event of a rodent sighting. "We're talking a New York City sewer-size rat."

"Ma'am, if you could please try to calm yourself, it would be best for the residents." The front desk attendant reluctantly lowered the soap opera magazine she'd been engrossed in before I came rushing up. "There are no rats at Bayou Gardens."

"I tell you, I saw a rat. It had a tail as long as—" I clutched the front desk as I faked a swoon because I really didn't know what a rat's tail looked like. Nor did I ever hope to find out. "Someone call for help." I was pleased when a small crowd of residents congregated around me. "I demand to see the manager. Or the owner." Still, the front desk attendant didn't move. She simply stared at me. "Call the State Board. They'll shut this place down if they know you're infested with rodents."

Apparently, the magic words were 'State Board' because that threat drew the manager from his back office. He bustled out into the lobby. "Hold on, hold on, there's nothing to worry about. Certainly nothing worthy of making any phones calls about." His eyes scanned those assembled until they locked in on me, the presumed source of hysteria. "Come back here into my office, young lady, and we'll sort this out."

I made a quick assessment of the man I believed to be Harold Lisieux. My best guess was that he was in his late fifties, had a penchant for nachos and beer if his paunch was to be explained, and he valued peace and quiet above all else. Which made him an easy mark.

"I most certainly will not," I cried. "Someone has to do something."

He held up his hands. "Right, yes, of course." He looked around the lobby. "Let's fan out and search the premises until we find—"

"No." My voice jumped several octaves. "Not that." Certainly not that, I didn't want anyone finding Fortune where she shouldn't be, doing something she shouldn't be doing.

Harold Lisieux spun around to face me. "Why not?"

Why not indeed? For a split second I wondered if it would be better to be in Fortune's place, but one look at my kitten heeled sandals reminded me that I wasn't dressed for whatever hijinks she was up to. "We're safer sticking together. Safety in numbers, and all that. Besides, we don't know how dangerous that rat might be. Right everyone?"

The chorus of agreement, no doubt inspired by sheer boredom on the part of the residents, was rousing and it encouraged me to keep going. "Who votes we call the State Board of Health? Don't you think the good folks in Baton Rouge would want to know what conditions you're being subjected to?"

I might have gone just a bit too far if the look on Mr. Lisieux's face was any indication. He slipped his hand under my elbow and attempted to pull me in the direction of his office but I dug my heels in and refused to budge. My mind raced as I tried to think what would Fortune do under the same circumstances. She wouldn't go willingly, that much I knew. Then neither would I. I jerked my arm free of his grasp and held both hands up in the air. "Can anyone act as a witness to this treatment? I'm being manhandled while a rat is running amok through this facility."

The expression on the manager's face left me with little doubt that he'd happily strangle me if he thought he could get away with it. "Now, that's just enough of that young lady," he thundered. "You'll need to come quietly to my office or I'll have security throw you out."

"Security ought to be rat hunting," a male voice called from the back of the crowd.

Chants of 'vermin, vermin' grew increasingly louder. I scanned the room, sensing a new energy from the crowd. I wouldn't mind coming back here to teach an etiquette class or two when this was all over. Not that I'd likely be welcome. Not with the manager threatening to call the sheriff's department on me.

"I wish you would," I retorted. "I'm certain Deputy LeBlanc would be very interested in living conditions here." What Carter would really think, I could only imagine. Maybe he'd think I was channeling Gertie. When it came to creating scenes like these, I'd learned from the best.

"There you are." I whirled around to find Fortune by my side. She turned a contrite face to the manager. "I apologize for my friend's behavior. She tends to overact, she's quite excitable."

"You call whipping the residents into hysteria, 'excitable'?" His face went red and he looked like he was just warming to the topic of what a horrendous human being I was.

"I'm sure she only saw a dust bunny," Fortune called out as she dragged me toward the door. "No one's going to report anything to anyone, but I'd better get her out of here before she really gets going."

We were out the front door before Harold Lisieux managed to compose a response. We were almost to the highway before Fortune turned to look at me. "Well, that was quite the scene."

"Thank you," I said in what I hoped was a humble manner. "I was just warming to my audience when you arrived."

"Oh. My. God. I cannot believe you and Ida Belle are actually related." She shook her head and hit the accelerator. "I think I'm going to buy one of those spit-in-the-tube DNA tests to double check."

I watched the vegetation whiz by me in a green blur. Frankly, I'd thought Fortune was going to be proud of me. Had she done much better? I asked her.

"Heck, yeah, I found something. I also spent a minute with Ida Belle to give her an idea of what to listen for tomorrow. Hopefully we can get them out of there within a few days."

I waited but she didn't offer any further details. Details to which I felt entitled to hear. "Did you find out something about Bull?"

She shook her head. "Not yet, but I will if he's connected to this whole thing."

"What whole thing?" I was truly lost.

"Trafficking."

I let this sink in for a moment. Good heavens, not again. "More drugs?" We'd just been through the wedding from hell that ended up busting a local drug ring.

"Nope, not drugs." She looked sideways at me. "Worse."

I frowned. What was worse than drug trafficking? I gasped. But no, that couldn't be. "You don't mean human trafficking?"

She nodded somberly.

I leaned back against the seat and closed my eyes. What in heaven's name had Gertie gotten herself into?

Chapter Seven

MY THOUGHTS WERE LIKE race cars buzzing around the international speedway that was my brain. I massaged my temples as Fortune drove back to Sinful in silence. She was more stressed out that I'd ever seen her. Was this because she was as horrified as I was? Or was she perhaps beginning to trust me and didn't feel the need to put on an 'I've got it altogether' air?

Either way, she *was* worried. Which worried me.

When we hit Sinful's Main Street, she slowed the Jeep to just under a breakneck speed.

"I assume we're heading straight for the police department," I said.

"You assume wrong."

"Then we're heading to your house and we're going to call Kase?"

She shook her head without bothering to glance at my way. Perhaps because she'd know I'd be wearing a disapproving frown? Which I most certainly was.

Surely my third question would be the charm. "We're going to call your friends at the CIA?"

Fortune made a strangled sound. Oh, right. I wasn't supposed to let on that I knew she was a federal employee.

"Your past co-workers," I corrected myself. "Surely, they'll know what to do."

Instead of answering, she swung the Jeep into an empty parking space in front of Walter's General Store. She switched off the ignition and turned to face me. "We're not telling anyone, anything, Stephanie. Not yet anyway."

"But, that's not right," I protested. "We've got to do something. Human trafficking is immoral. We need to report it."

"See, that's the funny thing about the morality police. They'll take a report but can do very little about most things. What we're not going to do is rush around making noise and tipping anyone off. They'll just move on, cover their tracks, and go further underground."

I nodded. She was right. "I just can't believe that Bull is involved in this. He's such a—" I struggled to find a polite way to call him a pipsqueak but I couldn't find another word that fit as well. "—pipsqueak."

"People said that about Hitler. Look what a nightmare it turned out to be when people underestimated him." She jumped out of the vehicle and motioned for me to alight as well. "We've got to be smart about this. Right now smart means radio silent."

We walked toward Walter's. "Shouldn't we at least tell Aunt Ida Belle and Gertie?"

Hand on the door, Fortune hesitated. "Gertie's the last person who should be told anything. But I did have a quick word with Ida Belle and tipped her off before I interrupted your very fine performance."

Touched, I fingered my strand of pearls. "You thought I gave a fine performance?"

She nodded. "I did. Now it's time to give another one. Let's go."

Walter looked up as we approached the cash register. The worry in his eyes told me that he knew Aunt Ida Belle had been injured.

"Hello ladies," he greeted us. "I'm glad to see you two. I've put together a box of goodies for Ida Belle that you can take home to her. I just got a shipment of her favorite beef jerky in." He smiled shyly. "Maybe it'd be better if I stop by her place after I close up. You think she'd like some flowers?"

"I think she'd hate them," Fortune said. "In fact, I know she would."

Walter grinned. "Yeah, she's funny that way."

I wondered how Fortune wanted to handle this. Were we going to tell him about Aunt Ida Belle's stay at Bayou Gardens?

The bells over the front door jangled as Carter entered the store. I stole a glance at Fortune. She looked happy to see him, yet weary at the same time. I didn't blame her. It was time to crank up the lie machine. Again.

"Hello Fortune, Stephanie," he nodded at us as he reached out to shake his uncle's hand. "I thought you two would still be getting Ida Belle and Gertie settled into their room."

Walter frowned. "Their room? Are they staying overnight in the hospital?" He looked between the three of us. "Or are they moving in with you, Fortune?"

"Neither, actually," I answered for her. "Both Aunt Ida Belle and Gertie are going to spend a month or so at Bayou Gardens."

Walter's shock registered on his face. "Bayou Gardens," he repeated. "But that's an old folks home."

"I believe they're called 'senior living communities' nowadays," I said. "But it's only temporary."

I watched Walter struggle to choose his next words. He was such a gentleman that he'd never curse in front of two ladies. But I sensed he was sorely tempted. "I can't believe Ida Belle agreed to that. Or Gertie either, for that matter."

Fortune looked at me and raised an eyebrow in a 'go ahead and lie your way out of this one' challenge. A challenge I accepted.

"Truth told, we didn't give them much choice," I said. "Aunt Ida Belle's wearing a cast and is under strict orders to take it easy, orders you know she won't obey. I'm sure you heard that Gertie hit her head. Someone needs to keep an eye on her in case she starts acting odd." I was now officially rambling but it was hard to know just where to stop. "It seemed a perfect solution to have the two of them rooming together so they could keep an eye on each other."

Walter folded his arms over his chest. "Seems like they could have done that at your place."

"Of course," I agreed. "If I wasn't going out of town."

He turned his attention to Fortune. "Why can't they stay at your place then?"

Fortune started to answer but I rushed in to help her out. "Fortune's going with me. To a convention. In Boston."

"You gals are telling me that you're going to head out of town when Ida Belle and Gertie are recuperating?" Walter looked at his nephew. "How much of this are you buying?"

Carter looked between us. "Precious little, actually. They're up to something."

Fortune was going to have to take it from here because I was in over my head and astute enough to realize it.

She held up her hand. "A little less judgment, Carter, if you don't mind. We're trying to make the best decisions we can under some trying circumstances. You know Gertie and Ida Belle well enough to know that trying to keep them quiet long enough to recover is no easy job." She turned to Walter. "Stephanie's blood kin to Ida Belle. If she thinks her aunt belongs in a facility for a few weeks, it's not my place to argue, is it?"

Wait, what was that horrible sound? Oh, right, the sound of me being thrown under the bus. Apparently, Fortune wasn't the world class liar I'd thought her to be if she was resorting to hiding behind me. Fine, I could take one for the team. "It's just until we get back," I mumbled apologetically.

Ten minutes later, with several days' worth of ramen noodles and a couple of six packs of beer stowed in the back of the Jeep, we headed back to Fortune's house.

"What's with all the ramen noodles?" I asked, for lack of a better place to start with my litany of a thousand-and-one questions.

"Well, we've got to eat something. Gertie's casseroles won't last forever."

I pulled a face. I didn't drink bear. And ramen noodles weren't a delicacy I'd yet ventured to try.

"Don't look at me that way," Fortune said. "You're the one who keeps talking about some convention in Boston. Talk about painting us into a corner. How's it going to look if we don't leave town now? Like we didn't want to take care of Ida Belle and Gertie at home, that's what. Not a good look for either of us."

Oh. She had a point. "Sorry."

"On the other hand," she said, her voice now more thoughtful than recriminating, "it might actually work in our favor if Bull doesn't think we're around. We'll just have to lay low somewhere while we figure out what he's up to."

I issued a swift and fervent prayer that we wouldn't end up on Number Two. I couldn't handle the stench. "In that case, we'll need to ask Ally to watch Priscilla for a couple of days."

"What we really need to do is get in touch with Big and Little."

My eyes widened. Big and Little Hebert were Sinful's contribution to organized crime. They'd proven to be helpful to us on more than one occasion, and were actually somewhat gentlemanly. Still, their involvement meant that our troubles were escalating to a whole new level. "This wouldn't happen to involve another air boat ride, would it?"

Fortune shook her head. "Nope. It's not transportation we need from them."

I really shouldn't ask. I knew I didn't want to know. I blew out a long breath. "What *do* we need from them?"

"Weapons. Lots of them. And remember, not a word to your boyfriend about this."

"TELL ME HOW YOUR DAY was, darlin'."

The warm rumble of Kase's voice should have made me feel cocooned and safe. Instead, my end of our conversation felt like a tightrope walk between two very tall buildings, sans a safety net. "Oh, you know, just another typical day in Sinful," I hedged.

He laughed. "That could involve anything from machetes to a boxing match."

"Hmmm," was all I said.

"Okay, let me make a few guesses. Did your day involve any high-speed chases?"

I pictured Fortune's Jeep tearing up the road between Mudbug and Sinful. But even though she'd been driving a good thirty miles above the speed limit, no one had been technically chasing us. "Sorry, that's a no."

"You have a conversation with any interesting characters?"

"I wouldn't say interesting exactly." There'd been the bartender at Spanky's, not to mention the whole rodent sighting discussion with the Bayou Gardens manager, but those were technically more bizarre than interesting. "Fortune and I chatted with Carter and Walter at the general store but that's about it."

Kase observed a moment of silence. Not a comfortable silence either. Did he know me so well that he knew I was lying?

"How was your day?" I decided to flip the question on him. As an FBI agent, surely, he'd have done something interesting.

"Nothing that I'm free to talk about, you know that, darlin'."

An awkward quiet filled the air space between us. I was curled up in a chair in my bedroom at Aunt Ida Belle's, dressed and ready for our visit to see Big and Little. Anxiety gnawed at my nerves like a little mouse with a hunk of cheese. I understood Fortune's directive not to confide in Kase about what we'd found out, but she didn't know what she asked of me. Silence and I weren't comfortable for long periods of time.

"How are Ida Belle and Gertie doing?" Kase asked.

Now, you would think this would be a simple, straight up question that I would be grateful to hear but it wasn't. How to introduce the topic of Bayou Gardens? Kase was likely to be as suspicious as Carter and Walter had been. My best bet was to say as little as possible. "They're both going to be fine. In time, and with plenty of rest."

"They there with you now?"

Something in his tone of voice warned me that he knew about their new living arrangements. Which meant I shouldn't lie, at least not about this. I never knew how exhausting it was to be duplicitous.

"No, actually, they'll be staying for a short while in a convalescent facility." Before he could pepper me with questions, I launched into a whole song and dance about how this was the best thing for them. I was out of breath by the end of my spiel, but I think I'd managed to convey that everything here in Sinful was normal. Well, as normal as things ever were in Sinful.

"Stephanie," Kase surprised me by using my Christian name instead of his pet name for me. "Whatever you and Fortune are up to, you'd better be careful. You hear?"

I neither agreed nor disagreed, nor did I divulge or deny anything. Instead, I wished him a goodnight.

Guilt needled me as I made my way out to the living room. Fortune looked up from her laptop. "What's wrong?"

I plopped on the sofa beside her. "I'm such a liar."

"Good. There's hope for you yet." She got to her feet and motioned for me to do the same. "Let's go or we'll be late for our meeting. Now, I want you to put on your proverbial dancing shoes so you can tap dance around the truth when we're talking to Big and Little. We're only going to tell them as little as we can in order to get what we want from them. I want you to play it cool, got it?"

I nodded. Play it cool. This I could do.

Chapter Eight

"YOU'VE JUST GOT TO help us, Mr. Hebert. Gertie's in the worst trouble, and we're afraid that she's going to end up murdered." I sucked in a lungful of air. "On top of that, my great-aunt is angry enough to commit murder. Not Gertie's, of course, but someone else's."

"Good evening to you, too, Miss St. James." Big Hebert motioned for his son, Little, to pull out two chairs for us. "Have a seat, won't you, ladies?"

Fortune shot me a look of pure annoyance. Okay, so I hadn't exactly played it cool, but I had kickstarted the conversation, hadn't I? I sat and folded my hands in my lap. My little outburst notwithstanding, I needed to mind my manners. "Thank you kindly for agreeing to meet with us."

Big nodded his head solemnly. "Of course. My son and I aren't impervious to a call for help from two damsels in distress. Are we, Little?"

I didn't have to glance sideways to know that Fortune didn't appreciate being referred to as a damsel in distress.

"Certainly not," the younger Hebert agreed. He stood beside Big, his hands clasped behind his back. His expression was as inscrutable as his father's was. "Of course, we hope that we might be able to assist you ladies, but ideally this will turn out to be a mutually beneficial transaction."

"What do you want from us?" Fortune asked, rather indelicately, to my way of thinking.

"You called us," Little countered. "What is it that you want?"

"Weapons."

I reached up and fingered my pearls. My, but hadn't the conversation turned from loquacious to terse awfully quickly?

Big steepled his fingers and tapped them together rhythmically. His eyes were locked on Fortune. I snuck a glance at her. She sat, outwardly calm, and met Big's gaze unflinchingly. I wondered if she learned that in CIA operative training. I'd have to ask if she could teach me that trick.

"Why weapons?" Big countered. "How many and what kinds?"

Fortune tackled the second part of his question first, rattling off the names that sounded like a Russian roll call. I wondered how she'd handle the 'why' part of the question.

"As for why we need them, Gertie's life is at stake."

Neither Big nor Little exhibited an outward reaction to the news. A credit to their mafioso training, I wondered?

"How precisely are weapons going to assist you in protecting her?" Little asked. "Has she been taken hostage?"

Fortune shook her head. "I wish. I'd feel far more comfortable if that were the case. She's gone and got herself mixed up with someone who isn't what he appears to be."

"Someone you don't approve of, I take it?" Big asked.

"It's not a matter of approval," Fortune said. "He's made one attempt on her life already. And the fact that he's taken out a life insurance policy on her means that he's going to try again."

Big made a tsk-tsk sound with his tongue. "We can't have that."

"No, we cannot," Little agreed. "Where is Gertie now?"

"Bayou Gardens," Fortune answered. "Ida Belle is staying with her. She'll do her utmost to keep Gertie safe but we need to eliminate the threat."

"Naturally," Big concurred. "You have our support there. But you didn't answer my question about why you need us to supply you with a stash of powerful assault weapons to eliminate one man."

"We're not going to kill him." I turned to Fortune, suddenly uncertain. "Are we?"

"No, we're not. But we need to use something as bait to get his attention." She leaned forward in her chair. "I want to offer him a partnership in a deal so lucrative that the life insurance policy he has on Gertie pales in comparison."

Our host nodded. "Thus, ensuring her safety. A smart move."

It was. If it worked. But we needed to move quickly. I shared Fortune's certainty that Bull was hatching another plan to murder Gertie. In my mind's eye, I could see Gertie sleeping in her bed at Bayou Gardens, snoring that funny little snore of hers, all the while completely unaware that Bull was advancing toward the bed with a pillow in his hands. A pillow he was going to use to smother her. "Can we borrow Manny?" I blurted out.

"Manny?" Little's eyebrows rose. "Whatever for?"

"To sit by Gertie's bedside until we trap Bull."

"Bull?" Big exchanged a startled glance with his son. "You're speaking of Bull Dozer?"

I nodded. "You know him?" Why was the little pipsqueak on the Hebert's radar?

"We do," Big said. His gaze shifted to Fortune. "We've recently heard that he's involved in an activity that we most decidedly disapprove of, truly deplorable. But I imagine I don't have to elaborate, do I, Miss Morrow?"

She shook her head. "I'm in complete agreement with you."

Big laid his hands flat on the table. "It's settled then, we'll loan you whatever weapons you feel would impress Mr. Dozer." He pushed a buzzer on his desk. "Manny, join us, please."

I clasped my hands together. "Thank you so much. We'll take excellent care of him."

Big held up a hand. "You misunderstand me, Miss St. James. Manny is going to help Miss Morrow with her weapon selection, nothing more."

Deflated, I sunk back in my chair. "We can't have him?"

Little shook his head. "There's no sense in tipping off Mr. Dozer at this point in the game. We can, however, send a less conspicuous associate of ours to keep an eye on Gertie and Ida Belle, if you wish."

I smiled my thanks. "Wonderful, now that's all settled, I feel so much better." I stood. "If there is anything we can ever do in return, please let us know."

Big heaved himself to his feet. "Indeed, there is, Miss St. James."

"There is?" That was fast. "What can I do for you?"

"We need a specific piece of information about a certain someone that we've been unable to obtain," Big said.

"Most frustrating," his son chimed in.

"Quite," Big continued. "But I would imagine your boyfriend might be able to provide the information we seek."

I stared at him for a long moment. "You want me to ask Kase for classified information on your behalf?"

Big shrugged. "Ask, snoop around, however you want to obtain the information. That doesn't matter to us." He took up a pen and scribbled a name on a business card and handed it to me. "We need the lowdown on this person within twenty-four hours."

I took the card and stared unseeing at it. He was asking me to use Kase's FBI resources to get him information? I couldn't, and I told him so.

Big's dark eyes narrowed. "Now, think carefully, Miss St. James, before you make a rash decision that would upset the little deal we've just brokered."

"Surely your friend Gertie's safety is worth the little trade off?" Little asked, his voice dangerously low.

I looked between the three impassive faces, not knowing if I should be enraged or frightened by what they were asking me to do. But what choice did I have? Gertie's life was on the line. I had to help. I nodded wordlessly.

This was all Bull Dozer's fault. And at this exact moment in time, I wanted nothing more than to wring his scrawny little neck with my bare hands.

I MADE IT ALL THE WAY back to Fortune's house before I lost my cool. Actually, I made it half way through a plate of Ally's chocolate chip cookies before I lost it. "Fortune, how could you set me up like that?"

She dunked half a cookie in her milk glass. "I didn't set you up."

"Funny, it sure feels like it. I can't betray Kase by feeding information he has to the Heberts." I swallowed hard, aware that I was choosing Kase over Gertie. Not a fair position to put me in. "It's not going to happen."

Fortune chewed thoughtfully. "Of course, it's not."

"What are you saying?" I demanded. "Back at the Hebert's, you encouraged me to agree to their terms."

"Of course, I did. Agreeing to their terms was the only way to gain access to the guns I want." She shrugged. "No big deal."

I stared at her. "No big deal? How can you say that? I consider betraying Kase's trust a very big deal." As I spoke the words aloud I realized just how much the thought of losing Kase scared me. I pressed my fingertips to my temples. My head felt like it was going to explode.

Fortune pushed the plate with the last remaining cookie toward me. "Let's pause for a reality check, okay? I never said you needed to betray Kase." She held up her hand to forestall my protest. "You just have to give the appearance of doing so. I mean, come on, how would *you* know how to hack into Mayeux's computer?"

I wasn't sure I appreciated her lack of confidence in my espionage abilities, although deep down, I shared it. "You mean we're going to double cross the Heberts? Isn't that dangerous?"

"No one's spying, and no one's double crossing anyone."

I tore my gaze away from the cookie that was calling my name. I was confused enough without adding more refined sugar to the mix. "I'm lost."

Fortune shook her head. "It's simple, Stephanie. You needed to promise the Heberts a tidbit or two of information on a person of interest to them in order to get their promise to loan us some weapons. If they choose to think that you needed to use under-handed tactics to gain the information, so be it. It doesn't mean you actually have to, right?"

My expression must have told her that I wasn't following.

"Just ask Kase for the information you need," she tried again. "Tell him what you need and why. No subterfuge necessary."

"You really think he'll just give me the information I ask for?"

"No. Not if he's half as good at his job as I think he is. But he'll likely come up with a little something you can give the Heberts."

I considered this. I liked the idea that I could be honest with Kase, this was good. But making the Heberts mad was a very bad idea. I verbalized this but Fortune didn't seem as concerned as I was about the possibility of ticking them off.

"It's probably time we quit depending on them for help anyway," she said. "No biggee."

Perhaps not to her. "But what if they come after me for not giving them what they want?"

"Easy, you just turn them in to the FBI. It's not that complicated." She watched me carefully. "Now, if you've got that all squared away in your mind, it's time we talk about the tricky part of our plan."

My eyes widened. "I thought that was the tricky part?"

Her expression told me she knew I wasn't going to like what came next. "Just hear me out."

What good ever came after those words? "I'm listening."

"So, here's the thing, I found a flaw in our plan to trap Bull."

"What kind of flaw?"

Clearly, she was uncomfortable. "My handler in D.C. doesn't think it's a good idea if I pose as an arms dealer. It might hit a little too close to home, based on assignments I've had in the past." She studied my face carefully. "Believe it or not, the black market for illegal arms is not as large as you might imagine. My colleague is concerned that if Bull does have any notable connections, and they hear about our deal, they might put two and two together and realize I'm hiding here in Sinful."

I nodded. "That makes sense." If it was true. There was still so much I didn't know about Fortune's background. But, for now, I was going to go along with her story. "So, we're going to find another way to trap Bull?"

She shook her head. "No, I still think the original idea is a good one. He's greedy enough to go along with it."

Fortune watched and waited for me to put it all together, but she waited in vain. Her words made no sense to me, and I told her as much. "Spell it out for me, please."

"In a nutshell, here's the plan. We're still going to lure Bull into giving up his plans to hurt Gertie by tempting him with the ability to make much more money selling weapons instead of people."

"We are?"

She bit her lip. "Well, technically, you are."

I did *not* just hear that. "Pardon me?"

"You heard me right, Stephanie." Fortune said. "You're going to broker an arms deal with Bull, not me."

Chapter Nine

"BUT I DON'T SPEAK RUSSIAN." I looked up from the hefty black semi-automatic weapon I was caressing with my fingertip. It lay nestled in a case, where it most definitely belonged. I'd never held a real gun. Which, to my mind, made me the worst possible choice to pose as an arms dealer.

"What's that got to do with anything?" Manny asked. "I've seen people dumber than dirt attempt to sell one of these babies."

I straightened my shoulders and looked him square in the eye. "I simply said I don't speak Russian, I never said anything about a lack of intelligence." My frosty tone was in sharp contrast to the sweltering warehouse where we stood around a table littered with weapons that sounded like a litany of past Soviet leaders...Malenkov, Brezhnev, Chernenko...I was beyond bewildered.

"Take it easy, Stephanie." Fortune looked up from the rocket-propelled grenade she was studying. "You don't have to know their names. You just have to appear confident enough that Bull believes you're a dealer. Trust me, once you start spewing numbers, you'll have him seeing stacks of Benjamins. He'll be hard pressed to remember you're even there. Greed is a powerful distractor."

It had better be. My life depended on it. "I still think I'm not the right person for the job." In fact, I knew I wasn't.

"It's a crazy idea you two cooked up," Manny said.

He was being far more talkative than usual, maybe because the Heberts weren't anywhere around. It was just Manny, Fortune, myself, and a table full of lethal weapons. This whole idea didn't sound any better today than it had last night when Fortune first proposed it.

"It's all about the bluff," Fortune said. "Don't tell me you haven't bluffed your way through many a situation back in Boston."

I considered this. She was correct, I most certainly had. "Well, yes, but no one's life had ever been at stake. Not to mention that none of the awkward meetings I'd had involved actual weapons."

She slapped me on the back. "Buck up and channel your great-aunt."

"I guess so," I agreed. I looked over the selection of weapons in front of me. It certainly seemed as if the die had been cast. I was going to have to find a way to convince Bull that I was an arms dealer, albeit a very unlikely one. I turned to look at Fortune. "What exactly am I supposed to get him to agree to?"

Manny closed his eyes and shook his head wordlessly.

Fortune's reaction was more patient. "You don't have to write up anything. It's not an Avon order. Just get Bull to talk. Imply that you know about his involvement in human trafficking. Hint that you're making a crap ton of money. Play up to his ego. You need a big strong man to join you, something like that."

I groaned.

"Oh, for heaven's sake, stop being a baby," Fortune said. "Every woman on this planet knows how to fake an—"

"Whoa," Manny held up both hands. "Stop right there."

"—to fake an interest, is what I was going to say." Fortune picked up the RPG and hoisted it on her shoulder. "Touch the weapons with confidence, look Bull straight in the eye, and make sure he knows you're doing him a favor."

"I am?"

Fortune blew out a long breath. "Yes, you are. You've already got this up and running, it's a real money maker, and he can get in on the action under one condition."

I nodded. "One condition. Right." I swallowed hard. "What condition?"

"That Gertie remains alive and well. Make her the deal breaker." She set the grenade launcher on the table. "Play up that you can trust him because Gertie does. Send him the message that her well-being is of the utmost importance. That should put an immediate end to his desire to kill her. That million-dollar life insurance policy will look like chump change compared to what you're offering him."

I nodded. Not because I understood or agreed with everything but because my throat was constricted with fear.

"We ready to fit her with a wire now?" Manny looked at his watch. "The boss said to make sure you have everything you need."

A wire? "Are you sure you shouldn't be the one to do this, Fortune? After all, you're far more experienced at playing a role than I am." I swept my arm over the table full of weapons. "Not to mention that you speak 'weapon' fluently."

"You'll do just fine, Stephanie. As long as you carry yourself with confidence, you're golden. Let Bull assume you know the names of the weapons, and if he calls you out for some reason, just stare at him like you can't believe how dumb he is." Fortune steepled her fingers and held them to her lips as she studied me.

I felt grossly inadequate under her scrutiny. It wasn't that I was unwilling to try to save Gertie. I *was* willing, but I was also terrified.

"I believe in you," Fortune said. "Look at all the speeches you give about frou-frou manners, and yet you somehow manage to keep a straight face."

Manny cleared his throat. "Look, Miss St. James, I don't mean to interfere here, but you don't have a choice. You gotta do this."

I nodded. "You're right, Manny. I can't let Gertie down."

He shrugged. "Yeah, well, there's that, sure. But don't forget that you promised the boss that you'd get him the information he wants. There's no backing out now." He clamped a beefy hand on my shoulder. "Let's get you wired."

"YOU KNOW, MANNY'S HANDS were surprisingly gentle for a man of his size." I stared at the white lines stretching out on the highway in front of us. "I bet he's got some stories to tell."

"Yeah, well, what we should be worrying about is your story for Kase." Fortune blew past a semi-truck at what felt like seven hundred miles per hour, although I'm sure she was only doing a hundred.

"What if he says no?"

Fortune pulled a face. "You've got him wrapped around your little finger." She shot me a quick look. "How serious are you two?"

"Serious enough not to want to alienate him with a request for classified information." I plucked at a loose thread on my linen skirt. "I've never felt like this about anyone before. I think I'm in love."

"You think?"

"No, I know. I am in love with Kase. He's incredibly smart, sweet, protective, and gentle with me, but I know he respects me too." I smiled. "He's funny, and he's good-hearted. He likes animals."

"Well, if he can tolerate that Persian of yours, I'd put a ring on it." Fortune grinned. "How's that for girl talk?"

I nodded approvingly. "Not bad."

We drove the remainder of the way to New Orleans in silence. I'd tried to assure Fortune that I could drive into New Orleans by myself but she'd insisted on accompanying me. I didn't know what she was thinking about, but I was rehearsing ways to butter Kase up for information. However things went down, I hoped they'd happen quickly.

We'd only had a very short visit with my great-aunt and Gertie in the morning. Frankly, neither looked well. Aunt Ida Belle appeared especially exhausted. Why wouldn't she? I was sure if she had any sleep at all last night, it was with one eye open so that she could keep an eye on Gertie. During our visit, Gertie had introduced us to Mary, the very nice volunteer, who spent most of the morning hanging around their room. My guess was that Mary was Big Hebert's plant in Bayou Gardens, for which I should remember to thank him later.

We arrived in the Big Easy in record time, thanks to Fortune's predilection for speeding. She dropped me off in front of Kase's apartment complex, refusing to come in. She had errands to run and wanted to grab a burger, so her story went. But before I could close the door, she handed me a black velvet drawstring bag.

"What's this?" I asked as I took it.

"Just a little something you might need." She pointed to my handbag. "Just slip them in your purse. You don't have to use them unless Kase gives you grief about leaving."

Something in the way she avoided my eye prompted me to open the bag. I drew out a pair of gleaming silver handcuffs. "Handcuffs? What on earth are these for?"

Fortune grinned. "If Gertie were here, she'd have some suggestions."

I raised an eyebrow. "I'm sure she would. But I'm asking you."

She shifted in her seat, an uncomfortable expression on her face. "Consider them your ace in the hole if you need to make a quick exit. We've got to get back to Sinful in time for you to meet Bull tonight."

I studied the handcuffs. "Am I correct that these are in lieu of drugging Kase like you did?"

"You're not going to guilt me into an apology." She took the cuffs from me, gave me a quick demonstration on how to use them, and then handed them back. "I gotta go, I'm double parked. Good luck." And with that, she gunned the Jeep and took off.

I tucked the handcuffs in my purse, certain that no matter what happened this evening, I wasn't going to need them.

But it turned out I was wrong. We did end up using the handcuffs, or more accurately, I ended up using them. Our visit started out wonderfully. The rush of genuine happiness I experienced when Kase opened his apartment door surprised me. Being with him felt natural, whether we were making small talk over a glass of wine or breaking bread together. I welcomed the chance to sit closely together on his sofa but I was on my guard. Getting swept away in a moment of passion would derail my plans for the night.

Everything was fine until the talk turned to what Big wanted. As per Fortune's directions, I didn't play coy with Kase or beat around the bush. I just flat out told him what I needed from him.

His first reaction was to frown. "Darlin', you know I can't give you that. My work's classified."

I traced the length of his snake tattoo with my fingertip. "I know, Kase. And I respect that. But I need something to give the Heberts to repay them for their help in setting Bull up."

He lifted a skeptical eyebrow. "I would have thought you'd advise a hand-written thank you note for such an occasion."

I pulled back from his embrace to look him in the eye. "This is serious, Kase. I can't go back to Sinful without something for them."

His eyes darkened. "I'll take you back myself and you just let me sort out the Heberts. No one will be needing anything by the end of the evening."

The steely determination underpinning his words spooked me. "I don't need to be rescued, although I do appreciate the offer. What I need is your support, your trust, and one tiny morsel of information to feed them."

His refusal was absolute, which I honestly expected. What I didn't expect was his insistence on driving me back to Sinful. "Listen, Stephanie, I'm not going to let you endanger yourself. Not when one call to Carter can offer Gertie the protection she needs. You've been playing with fire but I'm taking away the matches now."

"You can't prevent me from meeting with Bull."

"Oh, yeah?" His lips twisted into a smirk. "Just try to stop me."

Oh, why did he have to say it that way? It was almost as if he were asking for it. "I will if I have to. Be reasonable, Kase." My cell phone buzzed and I looked at it. "It's Fortune. She'll be downstairs in three minutes."

"I'm going down to have a word with her." Kase started to stand.

"Wait, please." My heart was thundering in my chest at the thought of what I was about to do, but what choice did I have? I slipped my right arm around Kase's neck to pull him in for a kiss while I reached into my purse with my left hand. When I was sure he was thoroughly distracted, I snapped one of the handcuffs over his wrist.

Kase pulled back in surprise but before he could react I snapped the other cuff around the wrought iron coffee table beside him. As he stared incredulously at what I'd done, I slipped the handcuff keys in between the sofa cushions. In a couple of hours, when I was meeting with Bull, Fortune could call to tell Kase where to find them. I shot to my feet and moved away so that he couldn't grab me with his free hand.

"Stephanie St. James, I swear to you, you'd better unlock these damn things right now." Kase's eyes blazed pure fire. One I doubted my words would easily put out.

"I'm sorry, Kase, I really am." I grabbed my handbag. "Just tell me something about this person the Heberts are interested in. Anything that will mollify them will do."

His answer was to let loose a string of profanities such as I'd never heard. He yanked on the cuffs but all it did was shake the lamp. I grabbed his phone from the table before he thought to.

"I'm going to leave this here." I laid it on the kitchen table.

"Don't you dare leave me like this," Kase demanded.

"I don't want to, but I have to." And then, before I could change my mind, I ran from the apartment, making sure to lock the door behind me.

Fortune was waiting at the bottom of the stairs. "How'd it go?"

"About how you'd expect."

"Well, did you have to use them?"

I nodded. "Clink."

She winced. "He'll forgive you. Eventually." She didn't sound wholly convinced. "Don't look back, but one of the Heberts' thugs is following us."

It took everything I had not to glance over my shoulder. "Why?"

"To make sure you're doing what you said you would, namely getting something from Kase."

As we drove toward Sinful and my meeting with Bull, I wondered if perhaps I'd gone too far. I needed to help save Gertie, but loosing Kase was going to be a high price to pay for doing so.

Chapter Ten

AS MY MEETING WITH Bull neared, my nerves were on the verge of shattering into a million tiny fragments. I was wired, literally and figuratively. "I don't think I can do this."

"You have to," Fortune said. "Bull's expecting you. It's too late to change the plan."

I paced the length of Fortune's kitchen. "Can we call Kase now and tell him where the keys are?"

She shook her head. "It's too early. I'm sorry, Stephanie, but we can't take the chance that Kase will rush down here and interfere."

I doubled my pace, which in Fortune's relatively small kitchen, made me feel like a fish swimming in circles in a tiny fishbowl. Our trip to New Orleans had been nothing sort of moronic. We'd accomplished nothing, unless you counted the obliteration of the one relationship that meant the most in the world to me.

Why was I following Fortune blindly? Go to New Orleans, she'd said. I went. Handcuff your boyfriend, she'd suggested. I had. What next? Shoot Bull Dozer between the eyes? Would I blindly follow her next order? No. Enough. I couldn't do this.

Fortune's cell phone rang before I could tell her I was pulling out. She wasn't twenty-five seconds into the conversation when I knew something was wrong. Deathly wrong if her ashen pallor was any indication. I held my breath as she asked a curt series of what, when and how questions.

"What's wrong?" I demanded when she hung up.

Her gaze locked onto mine. "It's Gertie. She's gone."

Gone. That one word sucked the air from my lungs. Gone where? Gone how? I struggled to articulate a question but couldn't.

"That was Ida Belle," she said, her voice shaky. "She's at Bayou Gardens still. She thinks someone drugged her, and while she was out, they took Gertie."

"What are we going to do?" The panic in my voice matched the terror that coursed through my body. Poor Gertie. Poor Aunt Ida Belle. She must be beside herself. "Should we head over there now?"

Fortune dropped her head in her hands. "Just give me a minute to think."

A minute? We couldn't afford that. "But Bull doesn't know why I want to meet with him. He's still focused on the insurance policy." Which meant every second we wasted talking was a grain of sand slipping through the hourglass that was Gertie's time left on this earth. I ran to the bathroom and, pardon my unladylike commentary, promptly lost my lunch. I splashed water on my face. *Pull yourself together, Stephanie.*

Fortune knocked on the bathroom door. "You okay?"

I opened the door and slumped against the doorframe. "I was sick."

"So I heard." She pointed to my chest. "At least we know the wire works."

I cringed. "Sorry. I panicked."

She studied me through narrowed eyes. "Are you going to be able to make it through your meeting?"

My eyes widened. "I'm still going through with it?"

Fortune nodded. "Yep, in fact we need to move it up if possible. Which means you need to call Bull. Not only that, you have to act like you don't know that Gertie's unaccounted for. Can you do that?"

Without hesitating, I nodded. "Give me five minutes to wash up and I'm ready."

It turned out that I only needed four full minutes to clean up. I grabbed my phone and pocketbook and followed Fortune out to the Jeep. "Can we call Kase now?" I asked as she pulled out of her driveway.

"No."

Why was I asking? Kase was my boyfriend, I was the one who'd cuffed him. And just why had I deputized Fortune as my commander-in-chief? Enough. As much as I'd grown to respect my great-aunt, Gertie, and Fortune, it was time for me to quit looking to them for direction. I pulled out my phone and dialed Kase's number. Only as I hit the green 'call' button did I realize that I'd moved his phone out of reach before I'd left. My heart sank. He wasn't going to be able to answer.

"You've got a hell of a nerve calling me."

I jumped as Kase's growl came through my phone. "How'd you reach your cell?" was the only thing I could think to ask through my shock.

"No thanks to you." He was quiet for a long moment, which I must say unnerved me far more than if he were reading me the riot act.

"Uh, Kase? I'm sorry about the handcuffs."

When he spoke after a long moment of silence, his voice was dangerously low. "You're going to have to do better than that." How I wished he'd added 'darlin' to the end of his sentence, but he didn't.

"In fact, you're going to get your chance as soon as I get to Sinful. See you in a little while."

He ended the call before I could respond. I looked sideways at Fortune. "Kase in on his way here."

She pounded the steering wheel. "Crap."

I bit my lip to keep from asking her what we were going to do next.

"So, here's what we're going to do next," she said as if she could read my thoughts. "You call Bull and tell him that you want to move your meeting up. Try to act as nonchalant as possible."

Nonchalant was the furthest thing from what I really felt but she was right. My hands shook so badly that it took me three tries to dial Bull's cell number correctly. But, to my relief, I managed to bluff my way through the conversation.

"Great job," Fortune said when I'd hung up. "You sounded like a girl scout selling cookies."

Oh, please. How hard was it to convince someone they wanted a box of Thin Mints? Nowhere near as hard as convincing someone to enter into an illegal weapons ring. In order to hold onto what vestige of sanity I still had, I focused on breathing in and out for the rest of the drive. I should have been praying, but my gut instinct told me that, in all likelihood, God was growing tired of the scrapes I kept getting myself into.

I shared the sentiment. In spades.

WITH MY STASH OF RUSSIAN weapons safely stowed in the backseat, I drove the Jeep toward the designated spot where I was to meet Bull Dozer. I'd left Fortune parked in Aunt Ida Belle's SUV less than a mile away. Far away enough to be out of sight but within the wire's transmission range.

Bull had readily agreed to move our meeting up when I'd implied that he'd benefit greatly from agreeing to do so. He'd snapped at the bait like a ravenous bayou alligator. What on earth had Gertie seen in the man? I shuddered.

Our rendezvous point was a road-side vegetable stand a couple of miles outside of Sinful. The choice struck me as odd when Bull had originally suggested it, but Fortune was convinced that it was used in his smuggling operation. I pulled up and reverse parked so that the Jeep was facing the road for an easy escape, just as I'd promised Fortune I would.

Bull sauntered over to the Jeep before I had a chance to get out. He wore a pair of faded denim overalls and a cocky smile. I hoped my expression didn't convey my absolute disgust. I forced myself to smile. I couldn't let on that I thought him a world class chump or that I knew Gertie was missing. "Hello, Bull."

"Good afternoon, Miss St. James," he said. "Fine evening we're going to have."

I nodded. "I'm sure. Thank you for meeting me." I gave a pointed glance in the direction of the make-shift lean-to that doubled as a vegetable stand. A solitary stooped figure was arranging a stack of corn cobs on a rickety table. "Are you sure this is a good place for a private discussion?"

Bull shoved his hands in his overall pockets and rocked back and forth on his heels. "Don't mind old Sampson," he said. "He keeps an eye on things out here for me."

I bet he did.

"I heard you was asking after me at Spanky's on Sunday."

"I was," I admitted. "I was hoping to find a way to speak to you alone. You and Gertie have been spending quite a bit of time together lately."

He didn't so much as blink at the mention of Gertie's name.

"I love Gertie," I continued on. "She's like family to me. But she's a bit of a straight arrow."

Bull threw back his head and laughed heartily. "Coming from the mouth of Miss Manners."

"Miss Prim & Proper," I corrected him. I should have let it pass but, honestly, this annoyed me more every time I heard it. "Yes, I'm a manners columnist. But that isn't how I make my money."

At the mention of money, Bull's laughter died away. "That so?"

I nodded. "I've had to develop a side business." I strove to sound confident and assured, as if dealing in weapons was as natural to me as wearing pearls. "It's been lucrative."

"That so?" Bull said again. I struggled to hide my annoyance at the repetition.

"Oh, yes. But recently I've run into a problem. Seeing as how you're a business owner, I thought perhaps you'd be able to help me."

Bull quit rocking. He crossed his arms over his chest. "Me a business owner?" He pulled a face. "Haven't you heard that I'm a professional good-for-nothing slacker?"

I nodded. "I certainly have. You've done an admirable job creating that illusion. But I know differently."

"Well, now, I'm sure you've heard all kinds of talk."

Time to up the ante. "It's more than talk, I've verified that. Your part ownership in Bayou Gardens intrigued me. I couldn't figure out why you'd invest money in such a dump, although I'm sure Harold Lisieux was happy to see an influx of cash."

"I don't know what—"

I held up a hand to forestall his denial.

"Don't insult my intelligence, Bull. I make it my business to know things."

"Such as?"

Fine, let him test me. I'd done my homework. "I know that in addition to being Harold's silent partner, you're running an import-export business." I stayed quiet while my words had a chance to sink in. "Quite an entrepreneur, aren't you, Bull?"

He didn't answer but neither did he continue with the hayseed shtick, which I took as forward progress. The sun wasn't quite setting, but it was dipping lower in the sky. Time to get this show moving along. "I admire your moxie."

"Why are we here?"

Finally, he asked. I was only too happy to tell him. "I am looking to expand my operation, and I need a partner who isn't afraid to take risks in exchange for great rewards."

The words 'great rewards' were like a slot machine lever that pulled up three cherries, judging by the way Bull's eyes flashed. "Rewards?"

I did my best to smile like a cat who'd discovered an unlimited supply of cream. "Such as you can't imagine, but the risks are great too." I twisted in the driver's seat and beckoned for him to come closer. "I brought a tiny sample of my wares with me just to give you an idea of what we're talking about."

Bull gave a low whistle when I unzipped the bag. A black rifle lay on top of the stack.

"It's a beauty," I said.

"That a Kalashnikov or a Dragunov SVD?"

I remembered Fortune's admonition to be cautious when it came to details. "If you don't know just by looking, then you're not the partner I'm looking for," I said as disdainfully as I could manage.

"It's a Kalash," he said. "I'm sure of it." He tore his gaze from the guns and met my eyes. "Let's just say we partner up, and there's cash in it for me. What's in it for you?"

"Distribution opportunities," I said, grateful for Fortune's coaching. "I imagine you've developed a sophisticated network. Your cargo is more difficult to transport than mine."

Indecision paraded across Bull's expression. Greed pulled him one way, caution another. "I don't know what you're talking about," he hedged.

Bull. He knew darn well what I meant. I attempted a nonchalant shrug. "You're not getting any judgment from me. After all, we're a country built by immigrants." It unnerved me that such a heinous mischaracterization of human trafficking could trip off my tongue. "But the items I buy and sell can't tell stories. That helps me sleep at night." I paused a moment. "Are you interested in talking numbers?"

"I might be interested in a potential partnership," is what he said.

I'm a greedy amoral bastard, is what I heard.

"Good. Let's set up a time to meet." I reached behind me to zip up the black bag. "It's getting late and I'm anxious to go check in on Gertie and my great-aunt."

He didn't flinch when I mentioned going to see Gertie. I confess this threw me. What sort of a human being could be so cold? Pure human scum, that's who.

"Can I get a ride with you?" Bull walked around the Jeep and hefted himself into the passenger seat before I could think of a rational objection.

"You're heading over to Bayou Gardens?" I asked.

"Why not? I'm as anxious as you are to see Gertie." He pulled the seatbelt across his chest and clicked the buckle in place. "Unless you mind?"

Mind? Of course, I minded. This wasn't part of the plan. But what else could I do but politely acquiesce? "Of course not."

Still, every instinct I had screamed that something was indeed very wrong. And once I'd pulled out on the road and was less than a couple of miles from the vegetable stand, Bull proved me right when he stuck the barrel of a gun into my ribs.

Chapter Eleven

"JUST KEEP DRIVING."

I slammed on the brakes. "I will not. Get out."

Bull's face reddened. He lifted the gun to my temple. "Don't be stupid. I'm telling you to drive."

It took every ounce of self-restraint I had not to reach up and swat his arm away. Even with a gun pointed directly at my head, it was hard to believe this was happening. Here I was, being held at gunpoint in the middle of a deserted road, all alone...except that I wasn't alone. That realization sent relief coursing through me.

Fortune was with me. Well, not technically with me, but at the other end of the wire. A wire that I was wearing to try to trap Bull into a confession. And how was I going to do that if I was sitting here silently? Precisely.

I began to drive, a moderate forty miles per hour. "You're making a big mistake, Bull," I said, choosing my words carefully. "I want you to point that gun somewhere other than at my head. If you're attempting to show me how tough you can be in a crisis, I'm impressed. But I'm also about out of patience."

He kept the gun trained on me. I glanced sideways, doing my best to look stern. "Call me crazy, Bull, but one of my prerequisites in a partner is that they obey my instructions."

"You need to listen to me," he nearly spat. "I am tired of taking orders from bossy women."

How I wish I could let Aunt Ida Belle have ten minutes alone with him. He'd be begging for mercy. "What do you think Gertie's going to say when I tell her about your serious lapse in judgment?" I glanced at the dashboard compass. We were heading due east. Sinful was due west. Bayou Gardens was northwest of our meeting place. Where was Bull planning on taking me?

"It's too late to care."

It took me a minute to realize that Bull was answering my question. "Why? Did Gertie find out that you are involved in human trafficking?" Wherever Fortune was, I hoped she was appreciative of my efforts to record incriminating information that would be admissible in a court of law. "Or hasn't she caught on yet?"

Bull's silence unnerved me. I'd have felt a thousand times more comfortable if he were running off at the mouth like the smug bastard I knew he was.

"Where is she, Bull?" I demanded.

"Fixin' to be six feet under." He jabbed me with his gun. "Keep running your mouth off and you'll be the next one pushing up daisies."

Gertie was dead? I slammed on the brakes again. "Dead?" I gasped for air. "Where is she?"

"Waiting to be buried." He smacked his free fist on the dash. "Drive, damn you."

He wanted me to drive? I could barely breathe. "Where to?" I managed to ask. My mind was spinning like a country fair pinwheel but I needed to keep him talking. "If you want me to cooperate with your plans, you're going to have to tell me what they are." Preferably loudly enough that Fortune could hear him and set up a trap. "Why are we heading east?"

"You don't need to know anything. Just do what I say."

I turned as far as my seat belt would allow me to look at him. A ripple of pure loathing ran through me. "Bull, I am not accustomed to taking orders." Haughty. Yes, I would go with haughty. Perhaps that was the anecdote to his cockiness. I needed to throw him off his game. Shake things up. Get the upper hand. "If you don't tell me where we're going, I'm going to turn right around and head back to Sinful."

What might have been indecision flashed across his face. Or maybe it was guilt. Or indigestion. I knew so little about this man. But he'd hurt Gertie, or so he said. I couldn't imagine anyone hurting her. Did a kinder soul exist? "How could you hurt Gertie?"

If the red flush creeping up Bull's neck was any indication, he was growing tired of my incessant questions. But he wasn't talking, and he needed to be if we were going to nail him to the wall. "Was it for the insurance policy?"

My words caught him completely off guard. "What insurance policy?"

A slight twitch above his right eyebrow told me I'd hit the bullseye.

"The one you took out on her life to the tune of a million dollars? Ring any bells?"

"I ain't telling you a damn thing."

"Big mistake, Bull. You need me. I'm Ida Belle's niece. She'll listen to me better than she'll listen to you."

"She's a stupid old bitch."

"Wrong on at least one count," I said. "Aunt Ida Belle isn't stupid. She's cunning. She doesn't suffer fools gladly, and she doesn't take prisoners. You need my help if you want her to believe that Gertie died accidentally." I thought of the wire I wore. "Unless you want to confess to her murder."

His response was to give me an earful of swear words. Under any other circumstances I would have simply walked away from him. However, there was the little matter of the gun pointed at my head. I undid my seat belt and turned off the ignition. Time for action. I held up the keys in my left hand, out of his grasp.

"What the hell are you up to, woman?"

"Unless you want me to pitch these into the dense foliage, I'd suggest you watch your language in front of me. I've had just about enough of your swearing." I jingled the keys. "Lower your gun immediately or you're going to be searching for the keys for the rest of your natural life."

"You throw those keys and I'll put a bullet straight through your brain."

I tilted my head to the side as if considering my options. "Frankly, that would be preferable to sitting here listening to your foul mouth spew nonsense." I could hardly believe what I was hearing myself say. Where was this false bravado coming from? "Then you'd have two dead bodies to account for and no one would believe for an instant that Gertie's death was an accident." I waited for this to sink in. "Goodbye insurance money."

"Aw, shit."

"Language, Bull. Language." How much longer could I stall? Why wasn't Fortune burning up the road to rescue me? "Tell me what happened to Gertie," I demanded.

"All you need to know is that she's dead."

"You're lying." Please God, let him by lying. I didn't want to live in a world without Gertie.

When he didn't answer, I pulled my arm back as if I were going to pitch the keys. "Last chance to work something out with me."

Bull didn't answer. Not with words, anyway. Instead he flipped his gun around and struck me on the side of my head with the butt of it so quickly that surprise and pain barely registered before everything went black.

"STEPHANIE, WAKE UP. I want you with me."

The disembodied voice floated through my mind. Gertie? Was that really her? I struggled to open my eyes but the resulting jolt of pain warned me it was too soon.

"For crying out loud, Stephanie, open your eyes."

It *was* Gertie. A strangled sob caught in my throat. "Gertie? Is that really you?"

"Take a look and see for yourself."

I forced my eyes open to find Gertie's lined face framed by a ray of bright light. Her smile was wide and her words were gentle. "You're okay, honey, you're safe here with me."

I blinked rapidly. "Is this heaven? Are we angels?"

Gertie's laughter rang out like Sunday church bells. "Shucks, no, sweetheart. What a hoot! No one's ever confused me with an angel before."

A curious disappointment filled me. The thought of being in heaven with Gertie was a comforting one. She'd be a fun angel, in a saucy, sassy sort of way. "Where are we?" I made the mistake of attempting to lift my head but the ensuing pain discouraged me from trying any harder. I did, however, manage to keep my eyes open. "You're not dead."

Gertie's smile faded away. "No thanks to you know who."

I reached up and touched her cheek. "He told me you were dead."

She shook her head. "It's going to take more than a broken heart to kill me." She took my hand in hers and gave it a gentle squeeze. "I need you to stay awake. Just in case you have a concussion."

"I'll try." My eyes had adjusted to the light by now. The brightness was coming from a light bulb that dangled from the ceiling by a single cord. "How long have I been here?"

"A couple of hours," Gertie said. "I was starting to get scared you were going to slip into a coma." She reached out and brushed the hair from my forehead. "You're going to have a terrible bruise."

"Where are we?" What I'd first taken for white fluffy clouds were, in fact, grimy white cinder blocks. I hoped God would forgive my faux pas, for surely the real heaven was delightful, not dingy. "I think I can stand up. We should leave before Bull comes back."

Gertie held up two fingers crossed into the shape of an X. "Don't ever say his name again in my presence. I never want to hear those four letters strung together unless the word 'crap' follows right after it."

"Agreed. But we have to get out of here."

Gertie shook her head. "No can do, honey. You're stuck here with the rest of us."

I frowned. "What are you talking about?"

"We're not alone, Stephanie." She slipped an arm around my shoulders and helped me to a sitting position. Aside from the initial rush of pain, it felt good to be upright. "This is Jean-Claude, next to him is Catheline, and the young'un is Michael."

I stared wordlessly at the frightened faces of a man, woman, and teenager. Collectively they put a human face behind the ugly words 'human trafficking'. I wiped away the tears that slipped down my cheeks. "Oh, my God, Gertie. These poor souls."

"I know, honey, I know," she comforted me.

I took a deep shuddering breath. I had to pull myself together if I was going to be of any help getting us out of here. I did my best to smile at the Haitians across from me but they, quite understandably, didn't respond in kind. My lord, but they must be frightened half to death.

I turned my attention back to Gertie. "What are we going to do?"

"Well, now, I haven't quite figured that out," she admitted. "This would be a good time for a one-armed Ida Belle and Fortune to come riding in to save us, huh?"

Fortune. Of course! "I'm wearing a wire, Gertie." The excitement and relief in my voice was palpable. "We can tell Fortune where we are." I hurriedly unbuttoned the top three buttons of my blouse. "Look."

Gertie leaned forward. "Honey, there's nothing there aside from the décolletage that your maker graced you with." She sat back on her heels and shook her head ruefully. "The dipshit must have stripped it off of you while you were unconscious."

Instinctively, I crossed my arms over my chest. I hated that man, truly I did. I tore my gaze away from Gertie and looked at the three people across from me. However they'd ended up here, it was by the ill will of Bull Dozer. They were the victims, not I. But still, the thought of Bull's fingers touching my skin made me nauseous.

Gertie snapped her fingers. "I've got it. We can be angels. Avenging angels."

I looked around the windowless room. Calling it a room was verbal generosity in the extreme. I'd been in nicer broom closets. Essentially, the chamber we were in was nothing more than a cinderblock box with one overhead light. "How exactly will that help us escape?"

Her smile faded. "That I haven't figured out yet."

"Okay, so here's what we know for sure. Fortune knew I was with...what's his name...and she must have heard that he had me at gunpoint before he knocked me out. So, we know she's looking for us."

Gertie nodded. "We also know that Ida Belle—" her voice choked up "—will stop at nothing to find us. Add in the Sheriff's Department resources once Carter hears about this, and we're going to be rescued. Guaranteed."

Unless we were killed first. The unspoken reality hung between us as precariously as the dangling lightbulb overhead. I stared up at it.

"Are we praying?" Gertie asked. "I suppose this is as good a time as any."

I looked at her and blinked until the spots disappeared. "Praying's good but we can do that after we've set a trap."

Gertie clapped her hands together. "A rat trap. Perfect!"

"Help me to my feet, please." Once she did, it only took me a minute to get the circulation flowing through my legs. I motioned for Jean-Claude to come stand beside me. I hoped my encouraging smile convinced him that I was on his side.

"Tell me what you want us to do," Gertie said.

"Better than telling you, I'll show you. Give me a boost."

Chapter Twelve

"RIP IT, SISTER."

"I'm trying, Gertie, but it's not giving." I yanked on the electrical wiring again.

"Just imagine wringing Bullcrap's neck with the cord," she called up encouragingly.

This was what I most appreciated about Gertie. In the darkest moments she never lost her enthusiasm for life. Or, in this case, for surviving long enough to gain revenge. "Okay, this one's for you, Gertie." With all my might, I pulled on the wiring. We'd already unscrewed the single lightbulb from the socket. All that we needed to accomplish now was to rip the cord off so we had something to tie Bull up with when he returned.

If he returned. The success of our plan was dependent upon him coming back for the Haitians. I had no doubt he'd be happy to leave Gertie and I here to rot.

"I've got it," I called out triumphantly as the wires grew slack in my hand. "Let me down."

"Jean-Claude, put her down," Gertie shouted.

"Gertie, he's not deaf. He just doesn't speak English, use your body language." Under normal circumstances this would be a dangerous directive to give Gertie but it worked, and I was soon standing on the cement floor.

"Now what?" Gertie asked.

"Now we wait for Bull-"

"Crap," she interrupted me. "His name is Bullcrap."

"Okay, now we just wait for him to come back. Once he does, we'll jump him and tie him up." We'd pantomimed this for the other three before we'd removed the lightbulb and they'd all nodded their understanding.

"What if he doesn't come back?" Gertie asked, giving words to my earlier concern.

"Fear not, he will." I wound the wire up like a lasso. "If not for these three, he'll at least need to produce your body to collect the insurance money."

"Insurance money? What are you talking about?"

Oh, for the love of red velvet cake, I'd said too much. "Never mind," I backpedaled. "Just believe he'll be back."

"Insurance money?" Gertie repeated, as if her mind couldn't process the implication. "Why would he have a policy on me?"

I reached out for her arm and once I found it, gave it a light squeeze. "The man is insane, Gertie. Let's focus on escaping."

She sagged against the wall. "He was going to kill me," she said in a monotone voice that was devoid of her usual spunk. "He never loved me."

I would have thought the fact he'd thrown her in here to rot would have already spelled that out, but, still, her delayed shock tore at my heart. I desperately wished Aunt Ida Belle was here. She spoke fluent 'Gertie'. She'd know just what to say. "He's not worthy of you, Gertie. Right now, we need to focus on survival, okay?"

"Right."

The ensuing quiet worried me more than if she'd dissolved in a fit of tears. "Are we all in our places?" I asked, as much to fill the silence as anything. "Gertie, move back away from the door. Stand here beside Catheline. Good, now we're all in place."

And so we waited. And waited. Just when I thought I was going to lose my mind, I heard the lock turn.

"Ready?" I whispered.

"Roger that," Gertie replied in a hushed tone. "Operation trap-a-rat is underway."

We all stood flat against the wall as the door slowly creaked open. The light from a flashlight's beam shone back and forth along the floor. I held my breath, silently willing Bull to enter the trap we'd set.

A human shadow played against the wall opposite the door. I held my breath. Just a few more seconds. I felt Gertie squeeze my shoulder, acknowledging that she too knew it was almost go-time. One, two, three...

In perfect unison, Gertie and I sprang toward Bull. As we'd planned, Gertie went in for the legs, tackle style, and I shoved hard against Bull's back. Within seconds, we had him pinned to the floor.

"Help me pin his arms, Gertie," I cried out. I couldn't believe the struggle that he was putting up. For such a pipsqueak, he certainly had some upper body strength. "Don't go easy, if we break his arms, so be it."

"What the hell?" Bull cried out as he twisted and turned. Oddly enough, he sounded just like Fortune.

Our Fortune. Who'd come to rescue us. I immediately loosed my grip on our captive.

"Oooff, stop," she ordered. "Quit kicking me, Gertie."

"Fortune?" Gertie's voice clearly conveyed her confusion. "What the heck are you doing here? You're ruining everything."

Fortune's answer was not fit to repeat here, but suffice it to say that it wasn't the kind of English that I thought our Haitian friends should be exposed to.

"Help me get her up," I instructed Gertie.

"Can someone turn on the damn light?" Fortune demanded after we'd hauled her to her feet.

"No can do," Gertie said. "We ripped the electrical wiring out so we could truss up the pig when he got here."

Fortune held up her cellphone, the flashlight app adding a tiny bit of light to our cement cell. "Didn't it occur to either of you that exposed wires are a fire hazard?"

Uh, no, actually it hadn't. "Of course, it did," I lied. "But we can talk about it later. We need to get out of here."

"Not going to happen," Gertie said, her voice oddly flat. "The door locks from the outside."

I didn't have to curse, Fortune did it for the both of us.

"Then Fortune will just have to wait for Bull with the rest of us," I said in my best camp counselor voice. "Six against one is better than five."

"Six?" Fortune shone the light around the small room. She lowered it when Jean-Claude held his hand up to block the light from his eyes. "Holy crap. I'd wanted to believe that I was wrong about Bull's trafficking. The scum bag."

"His name's—" Gertie began but I quickly cut her off.

"We can discuss that later. We need to go over our plan." Once again, I began to gather the wire to have it ready for when Bull showed up again. I shared our plan with Fortune so that she could get up to speed.

"What if he's armed?" she asked. "The gun could go off and a bullet in this small a space is going to hurt someone."

Irritation flared within me. "You're right, we should have thought of that. It would be so much better to wait to be executed rather than chance a stray bullet."

"Hey, don't shoot the messenger," Fortune countered. "But there's no sense in killing yourself while you're trying to save your life, is there?"

This I wouldn't dignify with an answer.

"Maybe you should turn off your light in case dipstick comes back and sees it."

Considering there wasn't a window, I didn't think this was worth worrying about. "Wait, where's Carter? Who's with you?"

Fortune switched off her light, which didn't bode well for good news. "I'm by myself."

"But surely you told someone that you were looking for us?"

"Not exactly."

I resisted the urge to scream, instead I pressed my palms into my forehead. "Isn't calling in for back-up standard procedure?"

"I'm not a LAPD cop, Stephanie. I'm a—"

"Librarian, right. I remember." The lack of light might well have hidden the frustration on my face, but it did nothing to disguise the sarcasm in my words.

Gertie clapped her hands together. "Hey, you two knock it off. You're not the only ones in this little pickle. I've been made an old fool of by the scum of the earth. And what about our Haitian friends? They're probably scared half to death."

Fortune and I mumbled our apologies. Gertie was right. It was time to focus on finding a solution.

"You don't happen to have cell service?" I asked, hoping against hope.

"No."

Just as I'd thought. "How about a knife?"

"Go fish."

"Save the games for later," Gertie whispered. "Someone's coming."

I opened my mouth to dismiss her claim as fanciful when I heard it too. Someone was unlocking the door. As one unit, we all shuffled back against the wall where we waited in silence for Bull to join us.

"You two wait for me to take him down," Fortune's voice was a barely discernable whisper. "Once he's down, get ahold of legs. Got it?"

I assume Gertie nodded her agreement, just as I did.

Once Bull stepped inside, everything happened in a flash. Fortune leapt at him, neatly taking him down. Bull fell so hard, I swear I heard the air escape his lungs.

"Got him, got him," Gertie chanted. "C'mon, Stephanie, get that cord around his ankles so the vermin can't escape."

I froze. Something was most decidedly wrong. "Fortune, you'd better turn your phone light on."

"Can't," she managed to say, sounding somewhat winded at trying to contain her thrashing prey. "Hurry up with that cord."

"But that's not—"

"Get the hell off of me," came the growl from under Fortune.

My heart sank. I was right, although I desperately wished I wasn't. But I recognized the cologne we'd purchased in Hawaii. "Fortune, that's not Bull."

"Damn straight," Kase growled. "All ya'all had better get the hell off of me or I'm going to fling you off."

Shuffling sounds and heavy breathing proceeded a beam of light from Fortune's cell. Starting from the pointed tips of his cowboy boots, the light traveled up Kase's muscular form, past his snake tattoo, before it reached his scowl of extreme displeasure.

"You're not Bull," Gertie stated the obvious.

Kase's frown deepened. He ran his hands through his hair as he surveyed us. "Who are they?"

I glanced at the intimidated expressions of Jean-Claude, Catheline, and young Michael. I smiled my most reassuring smile at them before turning back to Kase. "They're victims of Bull's trafficking."

Kase swore under his breath. He reached out a hand to me, which I gladly took. He pulled me close to his side and slipped his arm around my waist. I couldn't put into words how profoundly reassuring I found his presence. Until he spoke. "I haven't forgotten your little trick with the handcuffs, darlin'," he whispered in my ear. "As soon as this is over, you're going to answer for that."

"I'm going to turn off the light," Fortune announced. "There's no telling how long we'll need to preserve the battery."

We soon stood together in darkness, the only sound was our breathing. Kase's silence left me feeling strangely bereft. Why wasn't he reassuring us?

"Let's focus," Fortune said. "Mayeux, what's the word on Bull's last known location?"

"I've got someone working on that," he said, his voice terse. "Gertie, you okay?"

"I will be as soon as I'm back home in my bunny slippers," she said.

"Dozer didn't hurt you?"

Her hesitation was so brief that I don't know if the others picked up on it. "I'm as right as rain during a drought," she replied.

Except for my broken heart, is what I believed she left unsaid.

"Can we reschedule therapy for later?" Fortune asked. In contrast to Gertie's forced cheerfulness, Fortune's curt words gave voice to her frustration. "Mayeux, is someone with Ida Belle?"

"Yeah, don't worry about her. She's pretty much a prisoner in her room until we spring her."

"Oh, no," I groaned. "She's going to hate that."

"Too bad," Kase answered. "The last thing we need is one more person to keep track of."

"What did you tell Carter?" Fortune asked.

"What you should have," Kase responded. "The truth."

Carter! I'd forgotten about him. "He'll be here shortly?"

"Yeah, should be," Kase said. "So, let's agree not to jump him."

"Roger that." Gertie clapped her hands together. "And for God's sake, let's not let the door close either."

We waited for what felt like an interminable period but I doubt it was more than half an hour before we saw a flash of light from under the door. No one moved, no one uttered a word, but I don't doubt we were all experiencing the same galloping heartbeat as the door creaked open.

Chapter Thirteen

AN ODD GLOW OF LIGHT illuminating his body, Carter stepped into the bunker.

"Thank God," I blew out a long breath of relief. "We thought you might be that horrible Bull."

Something in the way Carter stood with his arms out to his sides and his palms facing up was my first clue that all wasn't well. The stumbling steps he took toward us, as if being pushed forward, was my second clue.

"Stop there, LeBlanc," Bull snapped. "Anyone else moves and I put a bullet between the good deputy's ears. Got it?"

In one swift move, Kase swept me behind him. I stumbled against young Michael. In what little light there was, I could see his anguish. The poor child. I was frightened, yet I knew all the people in the room and understood every word being spoken. How must he feel? I took his hand in mine.

"Listen, Dozer, you don't want to do this," Kase's voice punctured the silence. "You're in deep enough trouble without adding murder to the list."

"Shut up." Bull's shaky voice was in sharp contrast to Kase's soothing tone. "You're all screwing things up for me."

I shot a quick look at Gertie. Fortune had her arm around Gertie's shoulders. Whether to comfort her or to keep her from going for Bull's jugular, I wasn't sure. But, knowing Gertie's penchant for rebel rousing, I'm glad Fortune was at the ready.

"We're the ones who can help make things better," Kase countered. "The first thing you need to do is take your gun off LeBlanc. Then we can negotiate."

"Like hell I will." Bull snorted. "You fooled me once with Miss Fancy Nancy—"

I peeked out from around Kase's side. "Prim and Proper," I corrected him. "Not Fancy Nancy."

My correction was the straw that broke Bull's back. "Shut up. Who friggin' cares who you are?" He lowered his gun. "You're a lying, scheming bitch and I should just shoot you now—"

In a move that would put a gold medal winning synchronized swimming team to shame, Fortune, Carter, and Kase lunged at Bull. In the short tussle that ensued, they got him to the floor, wrested his weapon from him without a single shot being fired, and had him tied up like a rodeo calf in seconds flat.

"Let me at him," Gertie shouted. "I'll make him pay."

Thankfully Jean-Claude grabbed ahold of her before she could pounce. Michael and Catheline threw their arms around each, celebratory tears streaming down their faces. I wanted to join in, but a nagging feeling that all wasn't well yet pulled at me.

"What about the door? I asked. "Did it lock behind him?"

Carter was the first one to reach it. He pushed at it but it didn't budge. Kase stepped over Bull, but even adding his bulky might didn't help.

It was as if an explosion of curse words, in two languages mind you, detonated. I refrained from joining in, but I shared their dismay. I was going to need to powder my nose sooner rather than later, not to mention that a breath of fresh air would be most welcome. I glanced around at the dour expressions my companions wore. "Fear not," I said. "We've got sheriff's deputy here, an FBI agent, and a—" I noticed Fortune cringe, "—a librarian. Someone will come looking for us."

Someone didn't. Not for hours. I wiped the beads of perspiration (I don't sweat, not under the direst circumstances) from my forehead. I'd long ago given up listening to Fortune, Kase, and Carter postulate as to where back-up was. I didn't understand a single word that our Haitian friends were speaking. As for Gertie, she was seemingly finding some relief in ripping into Bull with all of her might. Heaven knew she had the right, and now was the time, before he went up the river. Or down the river, I'm never sure which way the water flows to a penitentiary.

Just when I thought I couldn't take another second of waiting, we heard several thumps from the other side of the door. Everyone, except Bull, jumped to their feet. Kase pounded on our side in return until the door opened just a crack.

"Anyone order a pizza?"

Aunt Ida Belle! The door swung open and we all rushed toward the fresh air.

"Watch the arm, watch the arm," Aunt Ida Belle warned as Gertie threw herself at my great-aunt. She looked us all over, from head to toe and back again. "Geesh, how many law enforcement agents does it take..." but her voice petered out as we took turns hugging her.

"Why aren't you at Bayou Gardens?" I demanded.

Her eyebrows rose. "I'd have expected a prettier thank you from you of all people."

I grinned.

"What the heck took so long?" Gertie asked, as several FBI agents swept past us with a defeated looking Bull.

My great-aunt swept her good arm out. "We're standing in the middle of a God-forsaken swamp. Both cell and radio reception dropped off a couple of miles from here. It was like looking for a toad in the bayou, I tell you."

"But you found us, thank heavens," I said. "Can we go home now?"

It was Gertie who answered. "I've had all the fun tonight that I can handle."

It didn't escape my notice that she was carefully avoiding looking at Bull. But, however brave she was acting, I knew she was going to hit an emotional wall soon.

Kase detached himself from a group of agents and came to join us. "I'm going to head back to New Orleans tonight with Jean-Claude, his wife, and son. We're meeting a translator there and need to get them debriefed and looked at by a doctor." His gaze swept our small circle. "Why don't y'all head home?" His pointed look at me let me know that we had a long talk ahead of us when he was off duty.

On our way over to the SUV that was going to take us back to Sinful, we stopped to exchange hugs with our Haitian friends. I didn't bother to contain my tears as I hugged them goodbye. I don't know that I'd ever been happier for anyone than I was for them, knowing they'd be heading back to Haiti soon.

AS WE ALWAYS DID AT the end of one of our little adventures, we ended up sitting around Fortune's kitchen table with a plate of Ally's cookies in the middle of the table. Aunt Ida Belle threatened us with bodily harm if we dared ask her again if she was feeling well enough to be out of bed.

"Keep in mind that I single-handedly rescued all ya'all from that cement box," she growled.

Well, she'd been accompanied by a cadre of armed law enforcement officers, but we let that slide.

"I'm sorry about Bull, Gertie." I bit my lip, unsure what else to say. I had no doubt that Gertie's heart was aching far worse than Aunt Ida Belle's arm.

Gertie shook her head. "Don't be. That critter was aptly named if anyone ever was. I wonder how his mama knew he'd grow up to be a pile of crap?"

My great-aunt, Fortune, and I exchanged glances. What could we possibly add to that?

"He made a fool out of me," Gertie said, sounding more vulnerable than I'd ever heard her. "Aww, heck. I made a fool out of me."

Fortune reached out and laid a hand on her shoulder. "Welcome to human race, Gertie. You were blinded by what you thought was love. Something every other woman has done or will do at one point in their life."

Gertie wiped away a tear. "I feel so stupid."

"I think your willingness to start a whole new chapter in your life is inspiring," I said.

Aunt Ida Belle cleared her throat. These types of discussions weren't her forte. "Look at it this way, at least you were brave enough to give what you thought was love a chance. Some of us can't even get that far."

Was she talking about her and Walter? Before I could ask, she shot me a warning glare. Clearly, she wasn't open to the question. Duly noted. For now.

"Looks like we're a bunch of losers in love," Gertie said. "Well, except for Fortune and Carter. Is he coming over?"

Fortune shook her head. "He's gone to arrest Harold Lisieux. But, yeah, love's a landmine alright."

Gertie looked at me. "And you and Agent Hunky. You lovebirds are fine, aren't you?"

Were we? "I'm not so sure." I reached for a cookie, broke a corner of it off, and stuffed it in my mouth. By the time I was finished chewing, they were all still staring at me. "There's the little matter of our promise to the Heberts."

I'd forgotten that Gertie didn't know about our visit to Big and Little until I saw her confused expression. Fortune and I took turns telling the story, complete with the part about my promise to betray Kase's trust.

Gertie gave a low whistle. "Whoa, that's ten times worse than the time you and Fortune drugged him."

"That was all Fortune," I protested. "I was an accessory after the fact."

"Just tell us you're not going to go through with it," Gertie persisted. "You could ruin the best thing that's ever happened to you."

I sighed. Gertie was right. Meeting Kase was one of the best things to ever happen to me. I loved him. And I could say the same thing about meeting Aunt Ida Belle, Gertie and Fortune. Yes, even Fortune. I think I was finally seeing what my great-aunt and Gertie saw in her. She was a good person. Librarian or CIA agent, it didn't matter. She was my friend.

"I can't try again, and not just because Kase is on to me now. It's the wrong thing to do." I said, my voice thick with emotion. I would never, under any circumstance, betray Kase's trust by stealing classified information from him to give to the Heberts. "I just don't know how to get him to forgive me for handcuffing him to a coffee table."

"We'll think of something," Aunt Ida Belle assured me.

"We've got this." Fortune gave me an encouraging smile.

"We'll feed Big and Little to the gators if it comes to that," Gertie said.

I looked around the table and laid a hand over my heart. "Thank you."

I didn't kid myself that this was going to be an easy situation to wiggle out of, but it was clear that Swamp Team Three had my back. Bless them.

A Note from Caroline

Thank you so much for taking the time to read this book. I enjoyed writing it and hope that you enjoyed reading it enough to pick up the next in my Miss Prim and Proper Series, Bayou Spirits.

Thanks to Jana DeLeon for her generosity in sharing her Miss Fortune world with other writers!

To learn more about my other books, please visit my website -

www.carolinemickelson.com[1]

I'd love to have you join my VIP Reader Newsletter so that you can be the first to hear about new releases, discounts, and contests. Join us!

---

1. http://www.carolinemickelson.com